Stories Of Adventure

Edited By Sarah Waterhouse

First published in Great Britain in 2021 by:

 Young**Writers**®
—— Est. 1991 —

Young Writers
Remus House
Coltsfoot Drive
Peterborough
PE2 9BF
Telephone: 01733 890066
Website: www.youngwriters.co.uk

Printed and bound in the UK by BookPrintingUK
Website: www.bookprintinguk.com
YB0472A

Foreword

Dear Reader,

You will never guess what I did today! Shall I tell you? Some primary school pupils wrote some diary entries and I got to read them, and they were **excellent!**

They wrote them in school and sent them to us here at Young Writers. We'd given their teachers some bright and funky worksheets to fill in, and some fun and fabulous (and free) resources to help spark ideas and get inspiration flowing.

And it clearly worked because **WOW!!** I can't believe the adventures I've been reading about. Real people, make believe people, dogs and unicorns, even objects like pencils all feature and these diaries all have one thing in common – they are **jam-packed** with imagination!

We live and breathe creativity here at Young Writers – it gives us life! We want to pass our love of the written word onto the next generation and what better way to do that than to celebrate their writing by publishing it in a book!

It sets their work free from homework books and notepads and puts it where it deserves to be – **out in the world!** Each awesome author in this book should be **super proud** of themselves, and now they've got proof of their imagination, their ideas and their creativity in black and white, to look back on in years to come!

Now that I've read all these diaries, I've somehow got to pick some winners! Oh my gosh it's going to be difficult to choose, but I'm going to have **so much fun** doing it!

Bye!

Sarah

Contents

Helena Hassini Kandeepan (5) 112
Makayla Osunmakinde (6) 113
Oakley Druce (6) 114
Eirene Bai (6) 115
Chloe Williams (6) 116
Rosie Webb (5) 117
Imaan Hawa Asif (5) 118
Olivia Cao (5) 119
Charlie Barnes (5) 120
Bobby Morris (5) 121

Cwmffrwdoer Primary School, Cwmffrwdoer

Kyron Thomas Haines (7) 122
Kylan Davies (6) 123
Ruby-May Jones (7) 124
Oakley Evans-Israel (7) 125
Archie Carter (7) 126
Summer Evans (6) 127
Rhys Needs (6) 128
Dafydd Pearce (7) 129
Sophie Flinn (6) 130

Fettercairn Primary School, Fettercairn

Kaiden Sinclair (7) 131
Helena Leon (8) 132
Zoe Anderson (8) 134
Mhairi Stewart (7) 136
Lois Watson (7) 138
Daisy Richardson (7) 140
Scott Argo (7) 141
Iona Young (7) 142
Thea Moore (7) 143
Emily Anderson (7) 144

Hereward House School, Hampstead

Joshua Taieb (6) 145

Hethersett Woodside Primary & Nursery School, Hethersett

Betsy Golby (7) 146
Jessica Pullinger (6) 147
Izzy (6) 148
Olivia (6) 149
Jinsi Cai (6) 150
Advaith Ravindar (7) 151
Xavier McCann-Williams (7) 152
Lillie (7) 153
Mia-Rose Wooldridge (6) 154
Thea Stevens (6) 155

Hydesville Tower School, Walsall

Maven Ngo-Hamilton (6) 156
Chevéyo Kadii Ngo-Hamilton (7) 157
Cataléya Ngo-Hamilton (5) 158

Pennyhill Primary School, West Bromwich

Harper Eagles (7) 159
Abdulla Abdow (7) 160
Finley Bowen (7) 162
Palak Rani (7) 164
Elizabete Kravale (7) 166
Mandla Dhlamini 168
Darcie Hunter (7) 170
Shubdeep Singh (7) 172
Cameron Lane (7) 174
Manjot Malhi (7) 175
Aarif Olaniyi (7) 176
Colt Bates (7) 178
Patel Aayush (7) 180
Jaya Madhar (7) 182
Logan Jones (7) 183
Emily Wang (7) 184
Ethan Guo (7) 185
Dominic Holder (7) 186
Sorana-Nicoleta Capiau (6) 187
Rosie Butler (5) 188
Scarlett-Mae Hughes (6) 189

Kyrun Bali (6)	190
Shamiya Barrett (6)	191
Amrita Shergill	192
Riza Nayeem (6)	193
Reuben Fuery (5)	194
Kawar Naunihaal Singh (6)	195
Phoebe Wall Boateng (6)	196
Agata Puzyrkiewicz (6)	197
Maddison Turner (6)	198
Oliver Stanislawski (6)	199
Rachel Morrison (6)	200
Imaan Olaniyi (6)	201
Toluwanimi Eniolorunda (6)	202
Jessica Garrity (6)	203
Leo Bolinski (6)	204

St Stephen's Kearsley Moor CE Primary School, Kearsley

Adam O'Doherty (7)	205
Jasmine Sheikh (7)	206
Ethan Fox (7)	207
Finley Pendlebury (6)	208
Paige Jones (7)	209
Teegan Thompson (7)	210
Lara Al Muqdadi (7)	211
Esme Thomasson (6)	212
Kaylee Ann Robinson (7)	213
Elijah Hayton (7)	214

The Priors School, Priors Marston

Johni Ashenden (6)	215
Arthur Jaques (6)	216
Pippa Hewins (6)	218
Ivy Wingrove (6)	219
Jarvis Owen (6)	220
Eliza Parratt (7)	221
Elias Barlow (6)	222
Henry Roberts (6)	223
Immy Threlfall (6)	224
Freya Van Vuuren (6)	225
Tilly Barron (6)	226
Cora Sadler (6)	227

Archie Cox (7)	228

Tongue Primary School, Lairg

Aurora Jackson-Hamilton (7)	229
Mia Martin (7)	230
Ruaridh Faccenda (7)	231
Magnus Holmes (7)	232
Lars Rueben Mackay-Buttress (5)	233
Struan Mackay-Shanks (6)	234
Olivia Findlay (5)	235
Lucy Mackay (6)	236
Elli Scott (5)	237
Paige Jones (6)	238

Dear Diary

On Saturday, I went to the Isle of the Lost. Mal came to greet me. Mal said, "Let me show you around. I've got friends called Evie, Carlos, Jay and Ben. I've got sweets and chocolate," Mal said. "I've also got drinks." So, Mal and I had sweet treats. Mal took a chest. "Eat some," she said. I opened the chest and ate the chocolate coins with Mal.

"It's smoky because of fumes," said Mal. I could see grey smoke coming from a house! Suddenly, a bridge appeared. Mal hopped into a limousine and we were on a new island! It was summer and we were in Auradon. Evie gave me a polka-dot dress. "It's beautiful!" I said, but with the barrier open, in came Maleficent the dragon! Mal made a potion and threw the purple goo over the dragon. The dragon shrank.

Elizabeth Byrom (5)

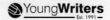

My Dear Story

Dear Diary,

There were two best friends since nursery called Hannah and Taymiyah. The two friends were sad because they had not been able to do much for a long time. They could not make friendship bracelets or go ice skating. Coronavirus, the monster, was spreading his virus everywhere.

Tay said, "Do you think Coronavirus the monster is going to stop spreading Coronavirus?"

"No, it has been here for two years," said Hannah.

In a flash of pearls, a fairy came.

"Who are you?" they asked.

"I am Kelly The Fighting Fairy."

"I do not believe in fairies," said Tay. "They are not real."

"They are," said Hannah.

"Where do you live?" asked Tay.

"I live in Cherry Village," said Kelly.

"We cannot fight, we have not got any magical powers," the friends said.

"I will give you two magic gems that can give you special powers. One has fairy magic, the other one controls the weather."

"Let's stop this monster!" they all shouted.

They found the monster, they used the weather gem, it made it so sunny the monster melted. It took three days to clean up. After that, Kelly's wand lit up... Out came a bunny called Maysa!

Hannah Haji (6)

The Unbelievable Fair

Dear Diary,

Today was the best day ever because my horse on the merry-go-round came to life! It all started yesterday at school when I got a merit. My mum said that I could go to the fair. "Really?" I said excitedly.

"You can go tomorrow," replied Mum.

The next morning, I woke up feeling very excited. I gobbled down my breakfast as fast as I could. At the fair, I met my friend, Kirsty, and we rushed to the merry-go-round and chose two white horses! The ride started and we both started to wiggle.

"What is happening?" I said.

"I don't know!" replied Kirsty. "Are they coming to life?"

Just then, our horses leapt off the merry-go-round!

"Argh!" we shrieked. Our horses galloped into Nutmeg Woods. We saw owls, foxes and squirrels! The squirrels prepared a lovely feast for us including marshmallows, cupcakes, biscuits and croissants!
"I'm absolutely stuffed!" said Kirsty.
"Same," I said. "Let's go home now."
We got on our horses and galloped back to the fair. They stopped at the merry-go-round and we climbed off them. Our horses winked at us, we smiled back and we couldn't believe what had just happened!

Lara Hangari (7)

Dear Diary

One day, I woke up and found that I had turned into a *dinosaur!* It was a bit of a surprise. I had olive-green skin, scales and a lovely crest.

I went downstairs to see Mum but she was scared and ran away. My dog, Poppy, hid under the table. "Don't be afraid," I said. "It's me, Matilda."

"But Matilda, you're a *dinosaur!*" gasped Mum.

"Don't worry, Mum, I'm only a herbivore," I said.

"Thank goodness for that. Let's have breakfast. I have some lovely lettuces," said Mum.

"No thank you, Mum, I'd rather look for lovely ferns outside."

So, I stomped outside and found some juicy ferns next to the River Welland. Suddenly, all the ducks started quacking and flapping. A blue head and a long neck rose out of the water. It was a beautiful plesiosaur! Then I

6

looked up and saw pterodactyls in the sky and a *massive* brachiosaur eating leaves from a tree. There were
dinosaurs *everywhere!*
Then a voice from behind me asked, "Are you a parasaurolophus?"
"I think so," I replied.
"So am I!" said the other dino.
All of a sudden, I felt much better.

Matilda Elliott (6)

My Friend, The Paintbrush

Dear Diary...

Something amazing happened at school today! When I picked up my paintbrush in art... *Whizz, pop, bang!* The paintbrush started talking to me. I couldn't believe it! The paintbrush said that she could grant me three wishes, so as the art lesson was nearly finished and I didn't want it to end, I decided that my first wish was that I wanted the lesson to be a bit longer... *Whizz, pop, bang!* The clock went back ten minutes. When the lesson was finished, me and the paintbrush went outside and there was a long queue to the slide, so my next wish was to make the queue go quicker and *whizz, pop, bang!* I was at the top of the slide! After we had lots of fun, I remembered that I had one wish left... Aha! I wanted to turn the paintbrush into a real little girl to play with me. *Whizz, pop, bang!* In front of me stood a young girl with paint splattered all over her body. She had long hair and freckles. We played all afternoon with the toy farm until it was home time. As the bell rang, the girl disappeared, but later that evening, I saw the paintbrush in my pencil case! I smiled to myself.

Goodnight Diary, I will write again soon.

Posy Hudson (7)

My Space Adventure!

Dear Diary,

My favourite teddy was Inky the alien because he could speak! At bedtime, we would talk about space. Also, the cool planets there too! There was Mars, Venus, Jupiter, Neptune and Saturn. We were always talking about them in my junior school. It was a grumpy school, so I told them, "Imagine you could go to all the cool planets and then you'd be famous!"

"Woah!" they would say.

One night, Inky said, "If we are always talking about planets, there's no point. We need to go there."

Hmm, I thought. "Yes, but when?" I asked.

"Now!" said Inky harshly.

"What the-"

"Quickly!" Inky said hastily. He put on my pink astronaut hat and set off.

"Have you got a spaceship?" I asked when we were just about to fly. But Inky's spaceship was small!

"I have big and small magic!" he said, making an odd humming sound.

After, we were in the sky. *Whoosh!* We arrived at the moon in the sky in no time. There was no gravity, so we jumped around. Then I heard something. Someone big and furry popped out of the moon holes...

Youran Lu (7)

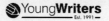

Easter Friendship

Dear Diary

It's me, Pinky, the rainbow flamingo. As next week is Easter, I've been looking for some Easter Eggs for my friends, Floey, Holls and Pinky-Winky (my little sister). I was searching for a few minutes when I saw a gigantic, ginormous, so-big-that-it-was-blocking-my-sight *rainbow galaxy chocolate egg!* It was definitely the one that I was looking for. But it was literally *massive!* I thought inside there would be thousands and thousands of miniature eggs just like it! I tried to lift the egg, but it was no use, so I flew high up into the sky, all the way home to ask my parents to help me. They weren't home. Ugh! I didn't know what to do. Suddenly, I saw Floey, Holls and Pinky-Winky. I asked them if they could please help and they replied that they were always happy to help me out.

We all went back to the egg centre. When they saw the egg, they went crazy shouting, "Wow, Pinky! Whoever this egg is for must be very, very special for sure!" We all lifted it up. I simply said - "You're right, it's for *you* guys! You're all so very special!" They shrieked with happiness. Easter rocks!

Sasha Wilkinson (6)

It Was Time For School!

Dear Diary,

I hadn't been to school for many weeks, because of Coronavirus. I felt nervous.

"Don't take me to school!" I cried, but my mum and dad said, "No!"

"But I don't want to go to school!"

"For the last time, you have to," said Dad.

When I got to school, I was in a very bad mood. "Please can you send me home?" I said to the teacher.

"No," replied the teacher. "It's playtime now."

I played 'forbidden forest'. This is how you play it. All you have to do is say, "Roger back, copy back, hey Oscar. Dingle dangle." Playtime was over. Lunchtime! The meat was too watery. I wished I could go home. *Sigh.* I wonder what I'll do? I've got to do something about school. So the next playtime, I was trying to think of a plan, but before I knew it, it was over. So, I said, "I don't want playtime to be over. Give me more time."

"I'm sorry, Luke, but I can't do that," said the teacher.

"But, but..." I stammered.

It was the afternoon. Why was I making eggs? Better luck next time. Grr!

Luke Spooner (7)

The Perfect Playdate

Dear Diary,

I hosted Kenna and Lila today. My mum bought a variety of pastry and coloured candies earlier on in the day from Madame Laura's corner shop. My brother screamed, "The preparation for your playdate is looking good!" My siblings, Kenna and I had finished painting our portrait on canvas before Lila joined us. Kenna is definitely a budding artist. Her painting was near perfect. Together, we all played musical chairs and the hopscotch game. Kenna won both games. Ah! I forgot to mention, Lila came with some yummy cheesy pizza and vanilla ice cream which we all enjoyed while we chatted. We talked about our school and our plans for the summer holidays.

We later watched the French version of Madagascar. It was a hit as everyone enjoyed it. We took our choice of pastry and candy. The doorbell rang, behold, it was Kenna's minder. I gave Kenna a big hug and bade her goodbye. Lila's mum arrived five minutes after Kenna left. My mum had a lengthy chat with Lila's mum which gave me more time to play outside with Lila. I enjoyed my playdate and look forward to hosting many more.

"What an eventful day!" I sighed.

Isioma Michelle Omeke (5)

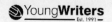

Ruben Thurairatmam's Birthday Diary

Monday 18th June

Today, it was my birthday. We went to London Zoo with my best friend Nathan. We stayed at the zoo for ten hours! We saw a large grizzly Gruffalo eating a hairy blue and green gorilla.

For lunch, we had Gruffalo crumble, it tasted hairy and furry. When I got home, we had a scrumptious Gruffalo cake.

Tuesday the 19th of June

I went to space with my best friend, Sam, from school. We were floating up in the air because there was no gravity. We were very lucky to arrive there by jetpack. We landed on planet snowball and saw an Arctic fox, a white polar bear and Rudolph the red-nosed reindeer!

Wednesday the 20th of June
When I got to Legoland with Jack, we made another Legoland with a swimming pool. It was so hot that the Lego melted, so we had to go to the shops and get some special Lego to make another Legoland so it never melted again.

Thursday the 21st of June
My brother, Milan, and I went to the funfair in Worcester Park. We were on a T-rex merry-go-round, then a huge spinning wheel. After this, we watched 'Hotel Transylvania' on the big screen and had delicious popcorn!

Ruben Thurairatnam (6)

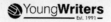
My Amazing Diary

Dear Diary,

The best day of my beautiful life was definitely my 5th birthday party. This is how it went...

In the morning, I woke up on a sunny day, full of excitement because it was my birthday! I was so excited, I got up and I changed into my gorgeous, glittery, violet dress with golden tights. I just couldn't wait for my family to sing the Happy Birthday song, so, after I changed, I quietly went downstairs because my sister was asleep (shh! Don't tell her).

When I went downstairs, my eyes couldn't believe what I saw. A banner saying 'Happy Birthday' and there were helium balloons of the number 5 everywhere. In front of me was a massive table full of delicious desserts. In the middle of the table, there was a pretty unicorn cake with a chocolate horn!

After everything was ready, the doorbell rang. It was my best friend with a sparkly wrapped present! When all my friends came, we played lots of games such as musical chairs. We cut the cake and popped the poppers! The confetti went everywhere! It was then the end of the party, so everyone
went home.

This was the best day of my life!

Arfa Tahir (6)

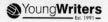
Dear Diary

Today, I was very excited as I was going to meet my friends, Iron Man and Spider-Man, at the space station. I woke up early, had breakfast and got dressed into my spacesuit. When we got to the space station, we realised that Evil Venom had followed us all the way. He was trying to spread poisonous venom everywhere! Spider-Man tried to save us by shooting his webs. Evil Venom then hit him with poison which ruined his suit. Iron Man intervened and quickly gave Spider-Man an iron spider suit from his emergency bag. Together, they defeated Evil Venom and sent him to Thanos' world, where he will never be seen again. We enjoyed exploring the space station without any disturbances after that. I think the space station is beautiful and magical.

Later, Iron Man took us out for pizza to celebrate defeating Evil Venom. I ordered pepperoni, whilst Iron Man and Spider-Man both chose Hawaiian, and we had ice cream for dessert. Iron Man invited us over to his house for some popcorn and a movie. I had an amazing time today. Mum picked me up from Iron Man's house at 6:30pm and we went home. I hope to see my two friends soon.

Ainsley Tsanga (6)

My Lockdown Experience

Dear Diary,

I am very happy now because I am going to school!

When full lockdown started, I made a birthday card for my teacher and cried a lot because I missed my friends and teachers, and I really hated lockdown. So, I sent a message to my teacher. She said she liked my drawings.

I drew some pictures that made me very happy. Then Mommy said, "Why is lockdown so sad?" So, I did many things to keep me and others happy. I made rainbow and heart window posters. I had fun while dancing ballet, singing, exercising, playing piano and dressing up. Home school was boring but I did well and I got a certificate. After, I did the 'superhero challenge' and I walked thirty-three miles in four weeks! I joined second language Zoom classes. I learned to play 'Mary Had A Little Lamb' myself and I learned cycling. So much fun!

Lockdown parties were also boring, so I made cake and a card for Daddy and Mommy's anniversary. But no relations or friends could come. So sad.
I learned many things in lockdown, but I don't like it and I hope no one liked lockdown.

Apshara Karuneswaran (5)

In The Forest

Dear Diary,

Today was an unusual day.

I was sitting in a tree with Erin and Isaac. We saw WhiteDoggy, BlackDoggy and Emmet the Lion going for a walk in the forest.

"I can smell a tasty bone," said WhiteDoggy and they started looking for it. A monster with three heads jumped out. One head swallowed WhiteDoggy. Another head swallowed BlackDoggy and the last head swallowed Emmet the Lion.

"Stop!" I shouted.

"No," said the monster and chased us away with its sharp claws.

We felt very sad, but then a bird started singing. "If stopping the monster is your wish, you need to find the magic fish."

So, we went to the seaside. A strange fish with wings flew out of the sea.

"I will help," it said and we went to find the monster.

The fish flew up the nose of a monster head. It sneezed and WhiteDoggy flew out. Another head coughed and BlackDoggy flew out. The last head burped and Emmet flew out. Then the magic fish put a sleeping spell on the monster.

We had a big party to celebrate with lots of tasty bones. We played musical statues and had a lovely time.

Jessica Kenny (6)

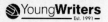
Dear Diary

Today was my 6th birthday! I got presents from Mummy and Daddy. I have a twin sister called Beth and she got birthday presents too like me. Me and Beth woke up early because we were excited about opening our presents. When we came downstairs, our presents were on the floor in a pile. I was so happy that our presents were wrapped up in wrapping paper with Elsa and Anna from the film 'Frozen'. My favourite present was a sewing kit because I love sewing.

Me and Beth were both at school in the morning and all our friends sang 'Happy Birthday'. Mummy got everything ready for our birthday party. Because of the virus, we couldn't invite our friends, so we invited our toys instead. We had yummy party food! We opened our presents before we played games. I won Pin the Tail on the Donkey and then I got a green gummy bear sweet. Mummy made us a cake each. Everyone sang 'Happy Birthday' and we blew out our candles with one big puff. Mine was a chocolate cake and Beth's was vanilla. I loved the icing because it was sweet. I had a brilliant day!

Molly McManus (6)

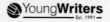

Portal-19

Tuesday 16th March, 2021
Dear Diary,
Oh my gosh! You will not believe what I've been through today! Let me start at the beginning...
It started out as a boring day in isolation, so me and my little brother, Rory, went outside to play football in the garden. Out of nowhere, we saw a cold shadow appear over our heads and a gust of wind shot out of something that looked like a portal. Suddenly, Mum's washing flew off the line and got sucked into the shadow. We decided to explore what it was, so I lifted Rory onto our football goals and I climbed up after to get a better look. These weird hairy creatures appeared, and reached out to grab me and Rory and pull us in!

Before our eyes, we saw flashbacks of us playing before the creatures threw us into roller-coaster seats and we could hear a voice talking. He was telling us that we had been picked to go on this special adventure. The voice stopped talking and we fell through the air into a room filled with buttons. Rory reached out to press a button as I shouted, "No!" But it was too late...

Harry Mann (7)

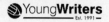

The Hidden World

Dear Diary,

As I sat alone in my room, a shimmery golden light caught my eye. The light was coming from an ancient-looking book at the bottom of my bookcase. The hard cover had a golden swirly design all over it. Even though my heart was thumping like a parade of elephants, I gathered my courage and opened the book. I was instantly pulled in!

I landed with a soft bump on a furry floor. I could see a girl wearing a golden headband. She had sea-blue eyes, long blonde flowing hair, and pointy ears. The elf, called Silky, told me that the magic book got the spell wrong and I needed courage to fight a very old but clever witch.

An idea popped into my head. I would ask all the elves to pour water on the witch from their windows. As the evil witch appeared, water came rushing down like a colossal never-ending waterfall. Instantly, the witch got soaked and started to melt. I heard all the elves cheering and clapping. Silky told me there was another secret way back to my bedroom.

I found myself waking up on my bed and I saw a golden headband next to my bedside table.

Resham Vadgama (6)

Corona Journal

Tuesday 5th January, 2021

Dear Diary,

I had two pieces of toast for breakfast. I am on day 5 of doing Veganuary so on one there was marmalade and the other peanut butter. Yum, yum.

We didn't go to school today because of the Coronavirus. Last night, Boris Johnson cancelled school. We have six weeks off school and are going into another lockdown.

I went back to school yesterday but most of my friends weren't there. But it was nice to see my teacher.

It is not very nice that people are dying. 830 people died today. Do you want to know how many cases of Coronavirus there are today? Well, if you want to know, then Boris Johnson, at 5 o'clock, will be on.

I hope that I can go to school soon. I have done homework like writing and phonics today. I did 'ou' and 'ay' words. I drew a picture of a pirate. It was really fun. I did 2 PEs - I ran up to the plastics factory and back and did a Joe Wicks workout. It was really cold. There was ice. My hands were freezing even though the sun was out.
I have had a wonderful time today.
Love, Jossy.

Jocelyn Kirk (5)

Kidnapped

18th February, 2021
Dear Diary,
I'm so bored in quarantine. What about you? Oh silly me - you can't be bored, you're just a diary. No offence.

Well, anyway, I was just in my room like... one, two... I think three hours ago, minding my own business (obviously) when *ding-dong!* The doorbell rang. Who was it? Why were they here? We weren't expecting anyone.

I opened the door and, in the blink of an eye, I was pulled and dragged into a... blue van? I couldn't see! Moments later, my head got hit... It went dark.

Woah... I felt a slight pain in my head. Sitting beside me were boxes upon boxes. What was in there? Did I just get kidnapped? If I did, they did a pretty bad job - the door was still open in the van. All of a sudden, *bump!* I fell out of the van. I felt weak, pain all over my body as I walked by the trees all alone... Before I knew it, I heard a few noises, then I fell.

And here I am, right now, continuing to write in you. I don't know how we... I mean *I* should feel. What will happen next...?

Mikel Obeng (7)

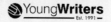

The Beach Trip

Dear Diary,
I have always imagined what a trip to the beach would be like, and thankfully, today my mum surprised me by taking me to the beach. We set out around 12 noon, loading the car with our multicoloured picnic mat, shovel, bucket, yummy food and fruity drinks. I stared outside the window as I rode with Mum, imagining what the day would be like. We got to the beach around half 1 and, behold, the beach was filled. *This is looking good*, I thought to myself. My mum laid our picnic bag out while I helped arrange our food and drink.
I introduced myself to Shane, a nice six-year-old boy, who had just begun making a sandcastle. He agreed for me to join him and together we moulded the most beautiful sandcastle ever. He must have made so many sandcastles in the past as he seemed so good at making them. My mum

sighted our joint effort and she came over to take our pictures while we squatted around the sandcastle.

We later went horse riding before he joined my mum and I for a snack. *Did Shane come alone to the beach?* I wondered.

Ifeanyi Nathan Omeke (5)

The Land Of The Dinosaurs

Dear Diary,

I had finally finished making my time machine and was excited for my friends to see my latest invention. I gave them some cola but, suddenly, one of my robots bumped into Louis and made him spill his drink all over the control panel.

Before we knew what was happening, the time machine sprang into life and we were travelling back in time.

We slowly opened the hatch and before our very eyes, there were ginormous dinosaurs with razor-sharp claws.

I looked around and realised that we were in a dinosaur nest. Then I remembered that the time machine looks like an egg. The mummy T-Rex must have thought it was hers and that it had hatched - she thought we were her babies! She made a strange roaring sound to call the other dinosaurs to come and look at us. There was over twenty of them. I was terrified!

I looked around to find the power key but it was nowhere to be seen! We have to get out of here!

Will I ever get back or am I stuck in the land of the dinosaurs forever?

Miles, the time travel explorer.

Miles Gelder (7)

The Secret Tunnel

Dear Diary,

Last night, I made the most magnificent discovery all on my own! But for now, I must keep it a secret.

I was home alone, playing with my pet wolf, Newa, all evening. My parents were on a very important shopping marathon and had left Newa to look after me as I was only eight. But Newa soon became drowsy and I too became exhausted. That's when I came up with the most insane idea to go out and collect loads of pebbles for Newa. I snatched my bag from my bed and skipped down the stairs and opened the back door to the gloomy garden. Newa stalked behind me. I went to a gigantic tree where the pebbles are usually found, and started to dig out some rocks and stuff them in my bag.

Newa joined in and actually started digging. She dug through the pebbles and into the soil. She didn't dig that much when we discovered a secret tunnel!

The soil sank into the hole, dragging Newa and me in as well. It was an unlit tunnel but Newa did try to help scrape the ceiling to get the moonlight in and, eventually, I was able to see...

Thigalja Uruthrasingam (7)

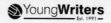
My Best Day Ever!

Dear Diary,
My best day ever in my life was my 5th birthday. Me and my family arranged a birthday treat and invited all my friends to the leisure centre nearby my home. A lady organised many games like 'Passing the Parcel, Musical Chairs and Simon Says'. I had great fun playing those games with my beloved friends. My parents bought a pretty vanilla cake, then I made a wish and blew out the candles and everybody sang happy birthday to me. Then I cut the cake. Then we all sat together and had the delicious cake and scrumptious vegetarian pizza and yummy milkshakes. In the end, my friends bought me so many gifts and I felt very special and enjoyed the day very much. I gave all my friends some return gifts too and we all dispersed saying "Goodbye!"

Finally, I reached home and was very eager to open all my gifts after my amazing birthday party.
I thanked my family for arranging such a wonderful and memorable birthday party. I always have so much fun on my birthday and I look forward to it every year.

Hansini Ariga (7)

Dragon At The Zoo

Dear Diary,

Today, I went to the zoo and I saw a dragon! And guess what? There was an alligator eating an ice cream and an elephant sucking up cheese! A crocodile having a cup of tea and a dolphin with a cupcake! And guess what? There was my sister standing on her head! There was a giraffe having a bowl of marmalade and a panda licking a spoon! A spoon, can you believe it! Dun, dun, dun!

What an amazing adventure, but the dragon set the zoo on fire. The animals all had to run out of the fire and, luckily, they were all in another part of the world. All that was left in the fire was a chicken eating a burnt cracker! *Peck, peck, peck!*

It is sad that the zoo burnt down and the chicken died, but it means I get to eat it. That chicken is now in my belly! We cooked it together and ate it for our lunch. Chicken for lunch and tea! It was actually pretty tasty. Yum, yum, yum!

Tomorrow, I'm taking a chicken sandwich with carrots on my picnic to the woods and I will build a log pile house. What a great day!

Jacob W P Bainbridge (6)

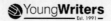

My Adventurous Day

Dear Diary,

Today was the best day ever! Let me tell you why.

Today, we went outside for a picnic after one whole year of sitting at home due to COVID restrictions. I could not sleep properly last night because of all the excitement. I got up early and started planning all about the picnic. We packed all the delicious picnic food and started our journey.

We decided that we would go to Animal Farm. During the car journey, I saw beautiful sceneries that I never noticed before. It all felt magical.

Finally, we reached the picnic spot, I fed the animals and their babies as it was springtime. It was the sweetest feeling ever. Suddenly, I saw a dog that was running after my little sister, so to save my sister from the dog, I threw the stick in the other direction so that the dog could catch the stick and we could run away.

My parents treated me with pizza for my bravery! It was indeed an adventurous day. Now I am tucked up in my bed, going to sleep with a wish in my heart that every day could be as wonderful as today.

Samarth Jain (7)

A Day With A Mermaid

Sunday 24th August

One beautiful, sunny morning, I woke up and looked out of the window. It was a perfect day for the beach, so I decided to go there. I packed my goggles, towel, swimming costume and other stuff. After I packed, I went to the lovely sandy beach. I built a sandcastle and swam in the shiny sea. When I got tired, I relaxed. I then heard a loud splash. I heard the splash again and again. *Splash! Splash!* Then I saw a sparkling tail. I tried to find out what was happening. Then I saw a gorgeous mermaid. She hid behind a rock because she was shy. I then noticed a fishing net tangled on her tail. I went into the sea and helped her. She was very grateful and happy to be free. She gave me a bright white shell. I thanked her. Then me and my mermaid friend swam and collected shells and pearls.

After, we were both very tired, so I decided to go back home. She was upset, but I promised her that I would visit her again, so we said goodbye. I ran back to my house and went back to bed.

Tanishka Wickneshwaran (7)

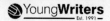

Sunday

Sunday, January 7th, 2600
Dear Diary,
It was Sunday morning. Me and Yo Yo Man went for a walk. Yo Yo Man has the power of a yoyo and all the men before him. He found the word 'Sun' on Sunday and thought it was the reason for the sun. Yo Yo Man has a shield to protect from all evil. We walked to High Square, a town protected by a dome made from a laser. Yo Yo Man thought the sun was falling. There was a massive fireball that landed outside the dome. The fire went out and what was left was a drone. The H.S.A. (Heroic Space Agency) were there to examine it to see if it was an alien. We were inside the dome for five hours whilst the H.S.A. made sure the drone was safe. We watched animated 'Intergalactic forces' on a screen in the zone. We had free food, a ginormous chocolate and strawberry

vegan doughnut cake with sprinkles and vegan ice cream!
It was safe to leave the dome at five o'clock. We left and played on our hoverboards and sniffed the flowers.

George Frank Gamble (7)

A Diary Of A Platypus (My Childhood)

Dear Diary,

I'm Wilma the Platypus, and I'm four years old. This is my story.

In Australia, I saw an aeroplane. I jumped very high to catch it! Then I went in a box and people thought I was a toy - I ended up in a shop! Someone wanted me, and one day she got to take me home. She loved me so much she couldn't leave me!

My family in Australia might be worried and sad, but they can trust that I'm okay. I saw my parents on the phone. Grandma comes to visit.

I started having toy friends: first was Chubby Cheeks. I got to have more and more adventures with my new family. All of them loved me! I went and tried new things, I went in the park, to lots of places! When I was in school, I learnt new things. I love my art homework, and I started going to ballet and gymnastics. I loved it! I was entered into competitions and shows.

Then it was Christmas! My brothers and sisters joined me, and I saw snow for the first time!

I promise to be good, because I am always good.

From Wilma.

Maddalena Cardelli (6)

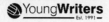

Diary

Dear Diary,

Today, I went to a park. We walked through a long path. I saw a bridge. We heard the loud noises coming from the birds chirping while we went past. We took a different path and saw a big tower. We couldn't go in because it was closed. Later, I reminded my mum that the car park closes at 7pm and there were only thirty minutes left. So, we decided to go and see the waterfall before leaving. We only had a small amount of time to watch, so we decided to go to the car park. We walked to find the exit but we were lost. After a while, we saw a man coming and my brothers asked, "How do we get to the car park?" He said we were on the other side of the car park and we had to run a long way.

Finally, we found the car park but it was closed. We stayed outside. It was getting dark. After a while, a kind lady came and asked why we were still outside. We told her what happened and she took us home. We got home and we said thanks to the lady for taking us home.

Dibisha Vasanthakumar

A Day At The Funfair

Dear Diary...

Yesterday, me and my friend, Adam, went to the funfair. We were so excited as we wanted to go on the speed ride, but instead, we paid to go into a deep dark cave. Upon entering the cave, we realised it was too dark to see. Luckily, Adam had a torch, so we could finally see! We kept walking and walking until we reached the end of the never-ending tunnel. There was a house, apparently with traps as it said that on the door so we had to be careful... We went into the house, only to enter into another tunnel, only this time it was darker. Still, we didn't give up, we continued to walk. It felt like there were rats running around us! Suddenly, there was a portal. We went inside and we landed on the moon... It looked spectacular, space looked so amazing, we were surrounded by stars and planets. We realised we were floating around. We reached a rocket, climbed in, then in a flash we were right back in the tunnel that we had been in to begin with.

Nasif Khan (7)

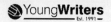

Space Adventure

Dear Diary,

Today, I went to space with my friend called James. He is seven years old and has short blonde hair. He is as tall as me. James lives in South Africa.

We used a rocket to get into space to the moon. The rocket was enormous and red in colour. It was as big as a helicopter. It was hard to get to James in South Africa and flying to the moon, but I enjoyed it.

We landed on the moon. It's white and grey in colour and round like a sphere. We drank some water from a very special glass cup. Suddenly, I found an alien! We liked the alien. The alien was a bit small in size. It had three eyes, eight hands and seven legs.

Soon, it was time to go back to Earth. I was sad but I had to go back home.

We flew as fast as lightning back to Earth. James went back to South Africa and I waved him goodbye with a smile.
I went back home. I miss James and the alien, but I know I will see them again soon. It's only a matter of time.
It was a joyful day!

Aydin Abdulazeez

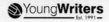

The Sad K

Dear Diary,

One day, in Letter City, the letter 'K' was walking down the path. He looked very sad. He loved knights who saved the princesses. Even though he was part of the team 'K-N-I-G-H-T-S', no one included him when they spoke the word.

"I am the first letter, why am I not included?"

The letter 'G' was passing by. "Oh, my dear letter 'K', why do you look very sad today?"

The letter 'K' told him why he was sad.

"Don't worry. Sometimes, they don't mention you. but remember, you are still part of the team. That happened to me too. See, I am there in 'K-N-I-G-H-T-S' and they have not mentioned me either!

You know, you are part of the team 'K-I-N-D' and even the team 'K-I-N-G'. You rule!"

'K' was happy.

'G' said, smiling, "So take off the hat of shame and wear a crown, o' king."

Aditi Variar (7)

My Lockdown Birthday

Dear Diary,

I am going to tell you about my 6th birthday.

This year, we celebrated my birthday at home because of the Coronavirus. I was scared that it would not be very special because we couldn't have a party. When I went downstairs in the morning, I was very excited to see all the decorations in the living room! I was so surprised when I saw the balloons everywhere. There were lots of presents on the table from my family, friends and neighbours. Lots of people sent me sweet video messages to wish me happy birthday.

I got to wear my beautiful birthday dress for the whole day and I had the best unicorn cake ever. My parents gave me a telescope for my present, so I can look at the stars and moon at night.

I really loved my birthday and was very happy in the end. I hope I will see a shooting star one day. Then I will wish that the Coronavirus will go away and I can visit my friends again and go to school.
Love from Tara.

Tara Narayan (6)

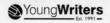

The Best Of Friends

Dear Diary,

Once upon a time, there were two friends, Mum and Vidhya (that is myself!). Both Mum and I loved to help people. Everyone loved us. One day, something happened... me and Mum were indoors when we heard a funny noise. I looked out to the garden and saw an alien. It was green and had yellow eyes. The alien looked sad. I felt it wanted to make friends. I told Mum about it.

"Oh! Poor thing!" said Mummy. "Let's go and help." So, we set off.

When we got there, the alien told us what his name was. I said to Mum that his name was Bob. Bob, the alien, spoke weird. Mum couldn't understand. So I had to translate what the alien was saying. Also, because of this alien language, Bob could not make friends.

"Oh dear, we want to be your friends, Bob!" both Mum and me said at once. Later that evening, we sat down to drink some tea. From then on, Bob, me and Mum were the best of friends forever.

Vidhya Bomidi (6)

Woolly Wonders Will Soon Be With Us

Dear Diary,
We are getting ready for our lambing season. Yesterday, Daddy and I put the tubby mineral buckets out for the ewes. They all came running across the field because they know the licks taste so good! Weenie and Daisy, my two pet ewes, were first over and shoved their heads straight into the tasty buckets. These minerals will help keep the sheep and the lambs inside them stay healthy until they are born. Soon the barn will be full of sheep, all waiting... We will wait with them. Then one morning, Daddy will shout, "Gina, first lambs are born!" and I will jump out of bed and run in my pyjamas to see if they are boys or girls and which ewe is the mum.

My job will be to feed the orphan lambs with milk in the special bottles we use with baby teats. The milk is yummy for the lambs but not for us humans, although Nell the sheepdog likes a dish if there is any leftover. Especially if it is still warm!

Gina Taylor (6)

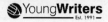

The Astronaut

Dear Diary,
Thursday, September 11th, 1999
It all started when I was lying on my bed and thinking about the dream I had last night. The dream began with me crowded by people as I was getting ready to go to the *moon!* It was my lifetime dream. I skipped into my rocket and went to bed.
Friday the 12th
I looked out the window and saw glittering stars, a sparkling moon and the darkest black hole ever. It was amazing. When I touched the moon with my feet, it felt rusty and *boom!* It exploded. I spent years banging and clashing until I had a sea-blue rocket. It was... amazing! I leaped into the rocket but stayed firmly on the ground. It was nice inside. I grimly thought it was dangerous but nice. It nearly had everything except my family. That was basically my life - it's all I want in my life!

Then I clapped on my back. Why, I fell into a nap! I saw a hawk on my little walk.

Ryan Gorman (6)

My Amazing Christmas

25.12.20
Dear Diary,
I had the most wonderful Christmas ever! It
was Christmas Eve and I listed every
spectacular gift that I wanted for Christmas.
Barbie dolls and a colourful drawing board
with a cute fluffy pen were top of my list,
and I was extremely excited to see what
gifts were gorgeously wrapped and placed
under our sparkling jingling tree. The day
had finally come, it was Christmas! The tree
was beautifully decorated, the glorious
presents were stacked nicely and the
delicious turkey was ready.
After we ate the scrumptious meal, I went
over to my presents and I found out I got
exactly what I wanted on my list. In fact, I
got a glamorous rainbow coat for my
Barbie as well! When we all finished opening
our presents, we all had so much fun
singing fantastic songs and playing
interesting games until we all got tired.

Overall, it was by far the most amazing Christmas I have ever had.

Tiffany John (7)

My Dream

Dear Diary,

Once upon a time, there lived a pixie called Thumbelina. She lived in a little village called Pixtown. One day, she went into a cave and saw a dragon. It was red and scary. Thumbelina was terrified. She had to fight the dragon. She screamed, "Help!" All of the princesses heard her and came to help her fight the dragon. Then, the superhero girls came to help too but someone was still missing. Then Mulan came. *Crash! Bang!* Mulan saved the day, but wait... The rest of the dragon family were angry. All of the princesses and super girls fought with the dragons, but they could not win. They all landed in the hospital. Everyone who worked in the hospital came to visit and looked after them. They soon got better. When the princesses and super girls felt better, they all travelled all around

the world. They were best friends forever...
Then my mum woke me up!

Liliana Charko (5)

Dear Diary

Today I went to the beach with Molly my sister, my mummy and daddy. It was sunny and warm. I wore my pink swimming costume. When we got there it smelled salty. I was so happy and excited because I love the seaside. Me and Molly built big sandcastles on the beach. Then we went in the sea. The sea was freezing cold! I liked splashing in the waves. After we got out of the sea, it was picnic time! We had hummus sandwiches, crunchy crisps, cucumber sticks and juicy tomatoes. For pudding, we had a gooey oaty bar. It was yummy! After lunch, we walked to get an ice cream from the ice cream van. I chose chocolate ice cream and Molly chose the same. It was delicious! After we had eaten our ice creams, it was time to go home. We packed up all the things and got in the car. Daddy drove us home. Me and Molly were tired, so we had a sleep in the car. I had a lovely day at the beach.

Beth McManus (6)

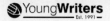

Bubble Bee

Dear Diary,
Today was a very strange day in Crazy Land because I met a magic bubble bee. Its bubbles were magical! If you went through them, you would turn into a bee! When I was in bed, I heard a buzzing sound above my head. I looked up and saw the bubble bee. She blew a bubble and I walked through curiously. Suddenly, a wing popped out from my back, and another. Now what was happening? Was I turning into a bee? A bubble bee I mean. Oh no, I heard my mum shout, "Breakfast is ready!"
I quickly buzzed into the kitchen... I was flying! How could I fly? I was a human, and humans cannot fly! I was very suspicious that day.
Tomorrow, I thought that if I found the bubble bee I could get it to blow a bubble and turn my mum, dad and sister into bees,

magical bubble bees. So I did and, after that day, we lived happily ever after. *Buzz...*

Catherine Greenhalgh (6)

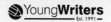

If I Were Abraham Lincoln For A Day

Dear Diary,

Today, I read about Abraham Lincoln and how he abolished slavery when he was president of the United States. I was inspired by his story. It made me wonder what I would do if I got the chance to become Abraham Lincoln for a day.

If that happened, I would bring a rule immediately that would stop people from cutting trees unnecessarily, stop racism and treat everyone equally. I would encourage everyone to help poor people so we can all live a beautiful life on Earth. I would urge everyone to protect Mother Earth and all of her beautiful creations. Animal poachers, burglars and murderers would be punished by chopping off their hands so they cannot commit the crime. I would strive to create a world where people look after themselves, their families, their neighbours, those in need and, most importantly, our planet, Earth.

Guru Kashyap (6)

My New Best Friend

Dear Diary,

Today, we went to the Jurassic coast of Dorset. It was really cold and windy. When we were having lunch, a huge fireball crashed on the beach. It made a *big* hole. I saw a beautiful rock in there and thought of bringing it back home with me. You never know, it might be precious. I saw Mary Anning on the beach, the world-famous fossil collector. I asked her to help me find what was inside the rock. She said, "Of course I will." We all went to her house and ordered pizza and started cutting the rock gently with the special hammer. Guess what was in the rock? It was a dinosaur skull! Mary was so proud of me and we became best friends. She even showed me her whole collection of fossils. I had the most amazing

day. Let's see if tomorrow is as wonderful as today.
Goodnight,
Love,
Vihaan.

Vihaan Gupta (6)

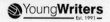

Safari Day

Thursday 1st April, 2021
Dear Diary,
Today, I was in Kenya with my family on a safari trip. It was a hot sunny day. When we came out of the lodge, I saw a green and blue lizard on the tree. It was very beautiful. We got into a safari Jeep to go around the park. I saw a lion hiding in the long green grass, giraffes eating tall trees, zebras running, a herd of elephants chewing the grass and one of them did a big poo! That was not nice to see. Then we saw an ostrich walking on his long, skinny legs, lots of baboons and a baby baboon looking at me, antelopes with long horns and rhinos in the water peeking at us.

When we got back to the lodge, I was very tired. I went in the swimming pool to splash at my family and then fell asleep on the lounge chair.

Tomorrow, we are going to Tanzania to see Mount Kilimanjaro.

Aania Bhamji (7)

The Magical Land

Dear Diary,
I went to Fairy Land with my best friend, Abigail, and this is what we saw: a fantastic potion lab to make spells, and a photo booth to take amazing pictures and lots of lovely shops too. That is what we saw, but this is what we saw that can move: hard-working fairies and flying unicorns and beautiful mermaids too! Me and Abigail went to an ice cream parlour because we were hungry and we love ice cream. The ice cream was really freezing! My flavour was mint choc chip and Abigail's flavour was the same as me as well as strawberry with chocolate sauce on top. Me and Abigail also went to the potions lab, and some shops and the photo booth.
Mine and Abigail's favourite thing was taking amazing pictures with each other. It all felt magical and it was the best thing ever!

Lucy Beaumont (5)

Dear Diary

It was a sunny day and I went to Disneyland with my family. I walked through the gates of the palace. Then I saw them the most beautiful thing of all. Sparkling dresses, red shiny lip gloss, wavy brown and blonde hair. There was a flashing light and rainbow glitter everywhere. I walked a bit closer and I saw them, the princesses, you know the ones that you read about in stories!
They came up to me and they spoke to me. It was all of my favourite princesses. I met Belle, Elsa, Anna and all of the other princesses you can imagine. One of them asked me if I would like to join them for an afternoon tea and I was so excited I couldn't speak.
I did join them for an afternoon tea in a magical restaurant, and I had a cream doughnut with sugar on top and whipped cream sandwiches.

Zoha Zahid (6)

My Half Term Diary

Dear Diary,

On Monday, I had a local walk and I walked into the park. Then I decided to come home.

On Tuesday, I went to Cassiobury Park. I spotted a route, I thought to go on it, so I went there. The path was flooded because there was lots of rain.

On Wednesday, I went to Cassiobury Park again but I had my wellies. I went where the path was flooded, we passed all the flood.

On Thursday, we went to Hyde Park. We crossed a bridge, then I saw a swan and it was trying to get my coat, but then I ran away.

On Friday, we went to Rectory Park. There were lots of people and I had a lovely walk.

On Saturday, I went to Horsenden Hill. There were lots of plants and we were following arrows so we did not get lost. Did you know that I was climbing a hill?

Neel Balar

Monster Friend

Dear Diary,

One morning, I woke up and I saw a monster under my bed! I was terrified because it grew bigger and bigger. It growled at me like I did something wrong. It threw my house around the place. My parents ran and the monster bumped downstairs and in my bedroom. They were terrified seeing the monster break through the roof! My parents and me ran outside, into the city, looking for a place to hide. Suddenly, loads of people ran outside of their houses and were terrified of the monster. They ran to hide in bushes and trees. The prime minister called for people to fight the monster who suddenly just wanted friends. The monster started to hug everyone, also the prime minister, and they were so surprised seeing the monster smiling and being very lovely.

Mila Mackessy (6)

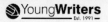

Astro Adventure

Dear Diary,
Today, I went through the magical portal in school that no one ever went in, that led me to the DSS Sauropod C Dinosaur Space Service in space! I met Teggs, Gispy, Damona, Arx and Blink. Tey told me all about their job and showed me their station. It was amazing! Then Teggs and the rest of his team had to leave me because they had to take care of a Fang problem! I've read about the Fang; they were nasty, evil and they meant trouble! Captain Teggs and his crew went off and left me in charge of DSS! I wasn't sure if I'd be able to do that, but I could. DSS led a massive battle with Fang and us. We won! When they came back, they even let me join in the celebration and I got a medal for helping. It was a great adventure!

Ryan Antonowicz (7)

Unicorn Land

Dear Diary,

Yesterday, I had an amazing trip with my friend, Laura. We were playing hide-and-seek in her house, in the attic, until we found an old chest. Inside it, we found a portal.

On the other side, we found Unicorn Land! It looked colourful. Everything was made out of different kinds of sweets. After we stuffed ourselves with all those sweets, we met a unicorn called Zoe.

For the whole day, we were riding on her back as she was showing us Unicorn Land. In the evening, we were tired and we wanted to go home, but we couldn't find the portal. Zoe took us to the Wise Old Unicorn who told us how to find it. Zoe took us to the portal and we went back home. It was an amazing adventure.

Megan Antonowicz (5)

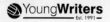
My Best Day Ever

Dear Diary,
Today it was the greatest day ever as it snowed! I love to play in and enjoy the snowfall. I could see snow everywhere. My garden was covered with snow, even the rooftops were covered in snow. It was a *snowy wonderland!*
The snow was falling like puffy white cotton. The wind was chilly and crisp. There were enormous snowflakes. When the snow stopped, we built a small snowman. It was really fun and my whole family enjoyed an amazing snowfight. Me and my brother enjoyed sleighing.
We didn't stay too long outside as it was freezing rapidly. Later, my mother cooked some hot soups and hot dinner to keep us warm. I slept early because I was tired.

Anayah Khan (6)

Dear Diary

Yesterday was the best day of my life, as I went to space with a Pokémon. We met a grey shiny rover called Zingea. Then we all had a picnic on Mars. We had a club sandwich with moon icing and special Mars lettuce.

We decided to do some stargazing.

Zingea said, "Look I can see the alien international space station." Baby Tim Peake was inside the ISS.

Next we all visited the blue planet.

"What's the blue planet?" asked Zingea.

The Pokémon said, "I don't know, we're about to find out."

We all found out it was Earth, we also found out there were aliens on Earth. It was the best day ever.

Om Joglekar (5)

Day At Drusilla's

Dear Diary,
Once upon a time, there was a girl called Little Red Riding Hood and a lion called Simba, and they had just got to Drusilla's and they were excited to see the penguins. But when they got there, there were no penguins to be seen! All that was left was a letter. And the letter said... 'Penguins have gone to Antarctica'.
They said, "We must find the penguins," so they went to Antarctica. They went by boat. Soon, they came to Antarctica. They knew that the penguins were yellow. It took hours to find the right penguins but they managed it. They went home by swimming and they all lived happily ever after.

Ella Fletcher (6)

Amazed During One Crazy Day

Dear Diary,

As I went to bed, I heard a croak in my moat! So, I sped under my bed and heard a roar by the door. I quickly ran downstairs to see a llama in pyjamas, a rock in my clock, a cow that wailed, "Wow!" and a clown with a frown! So, I went to hide in the bathroom and saw a red flower having a shower and a kangaroo in the loo.

After all that craziness, I went back to bed with all those amazing things in my giant head!

The next morning, at breakfast, there was an iguana eating my banana and a flea drinking my tea!

So I ran out of the door, screaming, "I can't take this anymore!"

Eden Lily Gambling (7)

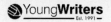
The Day I Went To Mars

Dear Diary,

Today, I went to Mars!

I built a rocket with cardboard, then cut a hole for a window and covered the rest with metal, and painted it red. Then I made the controls using plastic. When I had finished, I flew it to Mars and met an alien called Zob. Zob had three eyes and green and purple spots all over him. We made friends and played catch, football and basketball using bits of Mars, and Zob's friends joined in too. After a while, I was missing my friends and family, so I flew back down to Earth. Before I went, I promised I would see him again one day. It was the best day ever!

Aiki Fairburn (7)

The Adventures Of Cosmodoculus

Dear Diary,

There once lived a boy called Cosmodoculus. He had a dream. His dream was to be a heroic explorer. One day, when he was old enough, he went to the lake for a swim. While he enjoyed the cool water and the sunlight, a gigantic shark crept up on him! But Cosmodoculus did not hesitate! He had a speedboat with a water gun just for emergencies like these. He acted quickly! He jumped onto the speedboat and shot a jet of water right onto the shark's snout. It made the shark lose his way while Cosmodoculus swam to safety.

Coming soon... The revenge of the shark!

Om Kamat (6)

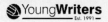

Dear Diary

On Wednesday it was the best day of my life as we went to the zoo. A monster ran out at me and said hello. I turned around to see who it was. I ran away then I realised it was lunchtime. Me and the monster became friends. We ate lunch together, we had a big cheese sandwich. When we'd finished eating we had chocolate. First we saw a Pokemon called Pikachu.
Next, we saw some tigers. After that we saw other animals.
The last thing we saw was a secret tunnel that led us home. We went through the tunnel and ended up a home and lived happily ever after.

Aditya Joglekar (5)

My New Unicorn

Dear Diary,

You'll never guess what happened today... I got given the coolest gift: a unicorn! She is so beautiful. Unicorn has got soft, bright pink hair and the fluffiest ears ever. Her hands and feet are covered in the colour silver. And lastly, a horn that is so sparkly sits on the top of her head.

I love her so much! We will do everything together. Tomorrow, Unicorn and I are going to go on an amazing adventure, just the two of us together. So, that was my *awesome news!* You are the best listener. I will talk to you tomorrow.

Bye for now.

Ridhi Jobanputra

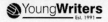
Dear Diary

Today, something amazing happened. I had fallen asleep when, suddenly, a soft scraping noise was heard at the front door. I ran to the door when a swish of wind came to me and swept me outside! The wind lifted me up. I have to say I was scared as I do not like heights, but all the same, it was amazing fun! Two people saw me and rubbed their eyes while I was gone.
The wind blew me back to the living room of my house where I walked to the door and saw a pup which was a blue husky. I also saw a note saying: 'Hope you like it'.

Aarabhi Hari (11)

Tia-Bella

Dear Diary,

I have a dog, her name is Tia-Bella. One day, when she was standing in her bed, I was pouring water in her bowl. The water bottle was soon empty, so I went to the 'Dogs Water Shop' to buy some more water. When I got back home, Tia-Bella had become an Arctic dog with pointy ears! Tia-Bella also had a bushy tail. We flew in the clouds! Then we flew back to the door of the house. My brother opened the door and I poured water in Tia-Bella's bowl. She drank and a glow surrounded her and me!

Oria-Sola Adewuyi (7)

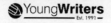
My Visit To The Moon

Dear Diary,
I had a little peek at the moon once. I have always wanted to go to the moon. So, one day, I went to the moon in my dreams.
I got to the moon in no time and I got to the moon very early. I felt like I was floating in the air! I made some friends, played, shopped and ate with them. Sadly, I had to go, so I said bye-bye.
Finally, I woke up, snuggled up in bed and I told Mummy I had a lovely day on the moon. I drifted off and had the same dream again.
Maybe I can go to the moon again someday.

Victoria Anyaegbu (6)

When I Was Sad To Leave School

Dear Diary,

When I came home and it was the Easter holidays, I felt sad because school is one of my favourite things.

I am so happy that none of my friends got COVID-19 so that I didn't have to go back to homeschooling. I am looking forward to doing fun things like playing tag and horses when I go to school. I enjoy doing my school work, especially literacy, maths, geography, history and PE.

I am looking forward to seeing which team wins the most house points and seeing all my teachers.

Henry Anderson (7)

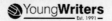

A Usual Day At The Lockdown Park

Dear Diary,
I went to the park today with my family. First, I went on the swings with my sister. A tiger from the zoo came into the playground and ate a child in one gulp! The mummy of the boy said, "I dare you to spit my son out!" The tiger refused to. Just then, the mummy turned into a fairy with a wand. She zapped the tiger into a slug! Her son came out all slippery and covered in slime. So, beware, at the park there might be a tiger lurking around or a fairy with a slug wand.

Michael Orfanos (6)

My Fabulous Birthday

Dear Diary,

I woke up and I jumped on Mummy and Daddy's bed! It was my sixth birthday! We had waffles for breakfast with honey! Then I opened my presents and was very happy to get a combine harvester! We packed a picnic and had soup in the rain! I love the rain!

We came home and we played the 'Mammoth Maths' game. We had a strawberry cake with a crab and a tractor on top because I love them. We watched a movie and then I went to bed.

I had a lovely birthday!

Albert D'Olier (6)

Monday

Monday 19th February, 2020
Dear Diary,
It was Monday and I went to the toy shop. I went on the number 17 bus. The toy shop was giving away free toys! There was a bus for sale on eBay, so I could get all of the toys on the bus.
I played with all the free toys and then I drove the bus around and then home. When home I went for a walk.
When back at home again, I cuddled the teddy bears and went to bed. It was bedtime.
The end of a fuzzy day.

Fred Gamble (6)

A Best Day In My Life

Dear Diary,

It was a lovely, sunny and bright day in August. My dad made a plan to go to Monkey Forest. Me and my brother, Shazim, were so excited and thrilled to see cute and naughty monkeys. When we reached there, I saw a countless number of monkeys! Some of them were climbing the trees. On one of the trees, Mum and Dad were holding their cute and tiny newborn baby monkey, and Mum was giving him milk.

It was one of the most marvellous days of my life.

Arshman Aamir (5)

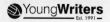

What We Did

Monday
Nanny drew hopscotch on the floor. I then got people passing to do hopscotch - it was fun while nothing is open.

Tuesday
We coloured a rainbow from our garden to next door's garden.

Wednesday
Dog walking the sausage dog of the lady who can't go out because of COVID.

Thursday
Cookie making with sprinkles was fun. I used the electric mixer.

Lillie Mae Crowe (8)

My Amazing Diary

Dear Diary,

Today, my mum told me that I could go back to school! I felt so happy. Lockdown was never-ending and it made me feel sad. I will miss the time I spent with my family when we were all home. I will always remember the snowman I made in the front garden. I named him.

I can't wait to see my friends and teacher again, I have missed playing with them and learning new things at school.

Speak soon,

From Ekam.

Ekam Singh (5)

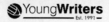

Dear Diary

I woke up in the morning and I was happy. I went to the park with my mum, sister and my aunty. We fed the greedy ducks. I wanted to ride my bike but the rear wheel was flat so I could not ride my bike. So, we went for a lovely walk instead. After our walk, we went back home. My mommy made some steak and it was delicious. My daddy got a Nintendo game for me. It is called 'Bowser's Fury and Super Mario 3D World'.

Navyd Salawu (7)

Someday

Dear Diary,
Someday I'll be gone, but before I go, I want you to know that I dreamed, I wished, I imagined tiny creatures leaping from their leaves. I want you to know that I imagined a different galaxy, away from the catastrophe that we created. I want you to know that, once, I bowed to the Guardians Of the Space Flow.
Before I go, I want you to know that happiness can be found, only if you keep dreaming.

Aadita Yadav (11)

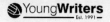

My Diary

Dear Diary,
I went to the moon! There were aliens. I saw
a chocolate river and alien superheroes.
"I like the moon," said Helena. There were
the aliens' families. My sister has long hair
and I have long legs and my dad has a big
nose. My mum has beautiful eyes.
I played football with my family. I felt really
joyful that my family were on the moon.

Helena Hassini Kandeepan (5)

My Dream 7th Birthday Party

Dear Diary,

On my 7th birthday, I would love to have a L.O.L. doll-themed party as I love L.O.L. dolls and they make me so happy. I would invite all of my best friends. I would want to eat a L.O.L. doll cake that is three tiers and is actually red velvet cake because I love red velvet cake! I want Queen Bee (a L.O.L. doll) because she is my favourite L.O.L. doll.

Makayla Osunmakinde (6)

Dear Diary

On Monday, I went to the beach and I got a slushy.
On Tuesday, I went swimming and the water was very cold.
On Wednesday, I went to the shop but it was closed.
On Thursday, I went to the park but there was a lock on the gate.
On Friday, I went to Africa and went on a trip to see the animals! I saw tigers and they were black and orange.

Oakley Druce (6)

Dear Diary

I was playing the Minuet in G minor by Bach, suddenly Chopin was knocking on the window. I told him to go to the front door. He was sobbing and told me why. He said Beethoven shouted at him.
Then Mozart came in. He was composing while walking and playing his magic flute. It healed Chpoin's sobbing. Then Vivaldi came and played the Four Seasons.

Eirene Bai (6)

The Scary Monster

Dear Diary,
Today, I went to the woods.
As soon as I got there, I saw a monster in the woods with sharp white teeth! But the monster was friendly and we had a picnic in the woods. Then it was time to go home, so I said goodbye to the monster.
When I got home, I went to bed and dreamed of jumping over giants.

Chloe Williams (6)

A Day With My Friend

Dear Diary,

I went to the park with my beautiful friend. It was her 6th birthday. We were very excited.

It was a fantastic day. I played on the roundabout. I drew in a book there. The sky was bright and clear. It was a good day. I loved playing with my friend and I got some cake that I ate in the car.

Rosie Webb (5)

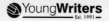

Dear Diary

Today, I have been on a lovely walk. I had an exciting day.
Tomorrow, I am going to the park. I enjoy spending time with my mum, dad and my sisters.
I am missing out on all the parties. After lockdown, I am going to have a big party with all my friends and family, with delicious food.

Imaan Hawa Asif (5)

My Riding Journey

Dear Diary,

On Monday, I went to the park with my family and best friends. We rode on bikes. We saw a pump track. I was a little bit scared the first time. But I did not give up. I wanted to play. I fell off and got up...

One hour later, I rode very well. I was so excited.

Olivia xxx

Olivia Cao (5)

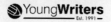

My Amazing Trip To The Park

Dear Diary,
First, we went for a one-hour drive to the park, and we played on the roundabout and had a picnic. We had cake and we bought a big ball for our trampoline! But it popped! I was sad. I looked through my big brother's binoculars.
It was a great day.

Charlie Barnes (5)

Dear Diary

Today, me and Esmè went to the zoo. We met a Pokémon, it was funny. We ate lots of sweets and played fun games.
After seeing the animals, we went home.

Bobby Morris (5)

My Amazing Time On The Moon

Dear Diary,

Last week, I went to the moon to find out if it was made out of cheese. I went with my friend, Ruby. First, we built the rocket. It was shiny and ginormous. We used it to go to the moon. As we were going to the moon, we saw a star. It was shiny and sparkly. After that, we went on the moon and started to look to see if there was any cheese. There was cheese! It was bright yellow cheese, so we used it to make a sandwich.

Finally, we went home because we were full up. The best part was the sandwich because the cheese was yummy.

Kyron Thomas Haines (7)

Cwmffrwdoer Primary School, Cwmffrwdoer

My Amazing Time On The Moon

Dear Diary,

Last night, I went to the moon because I found an alien that had crash-landed on Earth. First, I built a rocket. It was made of metal and it was shiny and strong. Next, I landed on the bare boring moon. There was nothing to see and nothing to do. Suddenly, we heard a strange noise. The alien recognised the noise. It was his happy family. Finally, I went home alone and left the alien on the moon.

I felt sad but I will definitely visit again.

Kylan Davies (6)
Cwmffrwdoer Primary School, Cwmffrwdoer

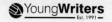

My Amazing Time On The Moon

Dear Diary,
Yesterday, I went to the moon with my friend, Kyron, to see some aliens. First, I went to the moon by very fast rocket. Next, we built some really big moon castles. Then I found an alien on the moon. He was green and very funny. Soon, I was jumping really high on the moon because there is no gravity there.
Lastly, we went home. It was amazing on the moon and I will try to go again to find my new alien friend.

Ruby-May Jones (7)
Cwmffrwdoer Primary School, Cwmffrwdoer

My Amazing Time On The Moon

Dear Diary,

On Wednesday, I went to the moon with my friend, Isaac, because we wanted to do some jumping. First, I found Isaac under my bed. He had been hiding there and was tickling my feet! Next, we flew to the moon. Then we started jumping. I went so high. Finally, we went home. I loved jumping high on the moon and I wish we could jump in the same way back at home.

Oakley Evans-Israel (7)

Cwmffrwdoer Primary School, Cwmffrwdoer

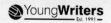

My Amazing Time At The Zoo

Dear Diary,

Last weekend, I went to the zoo with a monster. First, we went to see the lions. They were eating some meat. Next, we went to see the scary tigers. They looked as stripy as a hornet.

Finally, we went to see the huge elephants. They were having fun, squirting water out of their trunks. I had a great time. My favourite part was seeing the lions.

Archie Carter (7)
Cwmffrwdoer Primary School, Cwmffrwdoer

My Amazing Time At The Park

Dear Diary,

Last week, I went to the park with Leona to go on the swings. First, we played on the slide. We felt happy when we were sliding down really fast. It was fun. Next, we played on the swings. I hurt my tummy I laughed so much.

Finally, we played on the see-saw. My favourite part was playing on the swings.

Summer Evans (6)

Cwmffrwdoer Primary School, Cwmffrwdoer

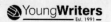
My Amazing Time On The Moon

Dear Diary,
On Friday, I went to the moon with my dad to play with aliens. First, I went in a rocket. It was big and red. Next, I played with some aliens. It was very fun and they had three eyes.
Finally, we went home. The best part was going home because I missed my mum.

Rhys Needs (6)

Cwmffrwdoer Primary School, Cwmffrwdoer

My Amazing Time At The Park

Dear Diary,

Yesterday, I went to the park with Logan to go on the climbing frame. First, we went on the slide. It was good and we went so fast. Next, we went on the climbing frame. We went really high.

Finally, we went home. I had lots of fun. I loved running around.

Dafydd Pearce (7)

Cwmffrwdoer Primary School, Cwmffrwdoer

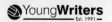

My Amazing Time On The Moon

Dear Diary,

Yesterday, I went to the moon with my mum to fly around. First, we flew to the moon. It was really cool. Next, we played on the moon. We played tag and it was really fun. Finally, we went home. My favourite part was playing tag.

Sophie Flinn (6)
Cwmffrwdoer Primary School, Cwmffrwdoer

Dear Diary

Last week, I was playing Fortnite and my friend magically appeared in my room! He looked older like he was from the future. They said, "Come with me," and I said, "No." I started Fortnite and ended up in the game. I went on a big golden boat that took me to a small island. There was a fun firework party going on and I joined in. I listened to Drake, he was performing on stage! I felt excited. While I was in the game, I met my cousin. They were sucked into their own game!
The fireworks stopped and the party ended. Lots of boats came to take everyone home. Me and my cousin stepped into a black portal and we ended up back in my room. I had a fantastic adventure!

Kaiden Sinclair (7)

Fettercairn Primary School, Fettercairn

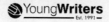

Dear Diary

Today, the most amazing thing happened! I was just playing with slime when I made an awesome slime unicorn. It took me to space! The slime unicorn looked like a rainbow and it had a swishy mane and tail. It was beautiful. Then I saw the Earth and in front of it was a space rainbow. Then something caught my eye. It was a glowing star. I felt amazed and, next, I ate it. It didn't taste good! Suddenly, I heard the sun sizzle and pop.

Then I hopped on the back of the space unicorn. It felt slimy. I was scared that I was going to fall off. It smelled like a sweet. I tasted the marshmallow that I had in my pocket, it was yummy. The unicorn ran away from me! Suddenly, I saw the slime unicorn queen, she was beautiful. I rode the queen back to my house where my other slime unicorn was waiting for me. Then I decided to keep them.

Finally, I went to bed but, while I was sleeping, they made me into a slime unicorn! When I woke up, I was in space. I woke up again and realised the last bit was a dream. I had an amazing time!

Helena Leon (8)

Fettercairn Primary School, Fettercairn

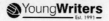

Dear Diary

Today, my family and I went to the zoo. At the zoo, I saw something unusual. It was a gummy bear giraffe! I named her Sugar. At once, she ran at me. I was so scared and closed my eyes and, a few minutes later, I opened them and I was riding Sugar! Sugar took me far away from the zoo. I closed my eyes again and opened them, and I found myself in a dark blue sea. I could see all the cute fish in the twilight zone. I could feel soft, fluffy, gummy bears falling from Sugar's body and I could taste saltwater. Suddenly, we heard a noise right behind both of us. It was a shark!
We swam as fast as we could. That was officially the most exciting moment of my life. We were nearly at the beach. Just before we got there, the shark bit off Sugar's toe!

We lay down and had a rest. We found a shell. It was dirty, so we rubbed it and a portal opened. We walked through and it took us back to the zoo. We would both remember this adventure with the bitten-off toe, and we laughed.

Zoe Anderson (8)

Fettercairn Primary School, Fettercairn

Dear Diary

Today, I was jumping on my trampoline when a bit of lightning struck and, in the blink of an eye, I was in space. I felt like someone was watching me. I heard a classical violin. Suddenly, a friendly, cute monster popped up in my face and said, "Hi, my name is Lilly, what is your name?" So I said, "Mhairi. So... Lilly, what is that smell?"
"It is the ice cream moon. So, Mhairi, why are you here?"
"I don't know," I said. "Lilly, how do I get home?"
"You must make a potion and I know the recipe."
1. One cup of milk
2. Two bits of lavender
3. Five hula hoops (the cereal)
4. Mix it all together.

So, we did the recipe. Once it was done, I drank a bit but it did not work. We made it again and it worked. I was back at my home. I had the most fun day in my life!

Mhairi Stewart (7)

Fettercairn Primary School, Fettercairn

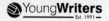

Dear Diary

Today, I had a magnificent day. I went to Magic Land where there were animals and sweets. I went to a park with cute animals and fairies. Then I saw a unicorn in the distance and the unicorn started running towards me, and it was my friend Holly the unicorn! I met her in the clouds.

After, she took me to the tree she was sitting under and told me to eat the leaves. I said, "No!" Holly said they were candyfloss, so I did eat them and they were good! Holly said everything in this world was sweets.

Then Holly took me to a wonderful feast. There were cakes, sausages, hot dogs, cookies, sweets, chips and crisps.

Finally, me and Holly went to her cosy house and watched a movie. It was very late when Holly and I went to bed. Holly had an extra

room, it was cosy in her bed. In the morning, she flew me home.
I had the best day ever.

Lois Watson (7)

Fettercairn Primary School, Fettercairn

Dear Diary

Today, I had the best day of my life!
I went outside to play. My BFF gave me some bubbles - magic bubbles. I opened the bubble pot, I said, "Wow!" Lots of bubbles came out like a volcano! I was shocked. Me and my BFF went in our houses. I went in my back garden, I played and played. All the huge bubbles were in the sky. I played with the bubbles all day! I made more bubbles until there were thousands. I jumped on the trampoline to try and pop them. When I popped them, fairy dust came out! I scooped up the fairy dust and mixed it with water. It made another pot of bubbles, so now I'll never run out.
I had the best day ever!

Daisy Richardson (7)
Fettercairn Primary School, Fettercairn

Dear Diary

Yesterday, I had a great adventure. Me and my brother found a big yellow square-shaped time hole. We ran into it very quickly. We ended up in the rainy jungle with the dinosaurs! We saw a herbivore, it had spikes on its back and tail. We ran up to it and climbed on its back. I held onto the smooth, sharp spikes. It took me to visit some more dinosaurs. They were smelly! When it was time to go home, I searched for the time hole. We found it on a dinosaur tree nest. It was guarded by a hungry dinosaur, so I had to sneak past. It saw me and chased me but I escaped.
I went back through the time hole and was back home. I had a good day!

Scott Argo (7)
Fettercairn Primary School, Fettercairn

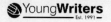

Dear Diary

Today, I saw a portal, so I went in it. I saw rainbows and it took me to Candy Land. I was far from home but there were lots of sweets! The floor was made out of sugar, the trees were made out of cotton candy. The trees were made from chocolate, it tasted awful! I saw lollipops, so I ate them. They were strawberry flavour. I went on a walk and saw two men, I asked if I could go in. They said, "Yes," so I went in and I saw a princess. She had powers! I asked if she could get me back home, she said, "Maybe." She did her magic and *pow!* I was back home. It was magical.
It was night, so I went to bed.

Iona Young (7)
Fettercairn Primary School, Fettercairn

Dear Diary

I had the best adventure ever! I went to a magical land of sweets and unicorns. I could see lots of candyfloss and lollipops of all different colours. I searched a long way. Eventually, I found a chocolate river. On my side of the river, there were lots of trees. On the other side of the river, there were no trees. Suddenly, on my side, a beautiful unicorn appeared, so I turned around. I wanted to ride on it.

I rode on the multicoloured unicorn! Then the unicorn opened a portal under my feet. I fell into it and ended up back home. I told my mum and dad about the adventure. They said, "Unicorns don't exist."

Thea Moore (7)
Fettercairn Primary School, Fettercairn

Dear Diary

Today, I went to Unicorns and Fairy Land. I never had an adventure, but today I had one and I was so happy. I could taste lots of cotton candy and orange gummy bears. They were delicious! I might make you hungry. I could see candyfloss trees, and unicorns with ice cream cones on top of their heads. They let me ride them. I thought that would be the last thing but no!
I saw the queen in a castle. We had a ball with tea. It was awesome. I was wearing a sparkly blue ball gown.
At the end of the ball, there was a portal outside. I jumped in it, I ended up in my bedroom.

Emily Anderson (7)
Fettercairn Primary School, Fettercairn

About Me

Dear Diary,

My name is Joshua Taieb. I am six years old and I like to get fresh air outside in the garden and the park, and I also like to read because I like the pictures inside the books. Nowadays, I am reading 'Harry Potter and the Prisoner of Azkaban' and it is illustrated by Jim Kay.

Joshua Taieb (6)

Hereward House School, Hampstead

Dear Diary

At the weekend, I watched TV about dogs and there was a cute, fluffy puppy on there. Next, I went on a pretend dog walk and I went to the park and I went on the slippery slide. After that, I had something to eat, it was so yummy. Then I got a pink Easter egg and a bunny, they were so lovely.
Finally, I went in the garden and played football and I won.

Betsy Golby (7)
Hethersett Woodside Primary & Nursery School, Hethersett

Dear Diary

Me and my brother made a cat war tank for a teddy. We made it out of cardboard and it took one hour.

Me and my brother went into my garden and went very fast on the swing and very high. I watched Henry Danger fight dangerous criminals with Captain Man. I ate peas and chips with sauce and water. I then went in the fun bath with my dolls.

Jessica Pullinger (6)

Hethersett Woodside Primary & Nursery School, Hethersett

Dear Diary

I went for a bike ride with my dad to the park. We went on the swings together, it was so much fun. Me and my dad played on the computer. We found some new slime on the game we played. I had a McDonald's. I got a Happy Meal and a Fruit Shoot. The McDonald's was really yummy. I went on a giant bunny for a ride, it was really fun.

Izzy (6)

Hethersett Woodside Primary & Nursery School, Hethersett

Dear Diary

On Saturday, I walked my ginger dog and went for a twenty-minute walk.
On Sunday, I went to Tesco with my mum and my sister and me and my sister got a drink. I got a bottle of Fanta and my sister got a strawberry juice. On Sunday, I did my homework and after my homework I made a salad. After dinner I had a doughnut.

Olivia (6)
Hethersett Woodside Primary & Nursery School, Hethersett

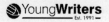

Dear Diary

On Saturday, I went to a place called The Pit, there were two swings, one made of a tyre and rope and the other made of rope. Then I saw Betsy at my house. She was with her sister on her pink scooter. I climbed an oak tree. When I was in the oak tree I ate some snacks. Next, I went for a bike ride then a walk.

Jinsi Cai (6)
Hethersett Woodside Primary & Nursery School, Hethersett

Dear Diary

First, I did some target practice. At first I was really bad, but I was really good after two days.
Last Monday, I got a nice coloured umbrella, I like it a lot.
The third thing I did was I played a cricket match against my dad and I won very quickly!

Advaith Ravindar (7)

Hethersett Woodside Primary & Nursery School, Hethersett

Dear Diary

Last weekend, I went on an hour and fifteen minutes Pokémon hunt. First I caught a wild Stunfish with an Ultra Ball and Pinap Berry. Second, I caught a wild and stubborn Froakie. I used a Pokéball and Nanab Berry to catch the Froakie.

Xavier McCann-Williams (7)
Hethersett Woodside Primary & Nursery School, Hethersett

Dear Diary

On Saturday, I went on my bike to the park with my wonderful dad and my wonderful dog and my wonderful stepmum.
On Sunday I went into the garden with my dog Mollie and my stepmum, Alice. We played ball in the garden.

Lillie (7)
Hethersett Woodside Primary & Nursery School, Hethersett

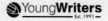

Dear Diary

I ate a lot of chocolate. I walked to the park. I went on the swing. I went on the slide and waited for my sisters at the bottom. Then I went down the slide backwards. The next day I got my new puppy!

Mia-Rose Wooldridge (6)
Hethersett Woodside Primary & Nursery School, Hethersett

Dear Diary

I went outside. I went on the trampoline. I went on my Xbox, it was fun. I made slime, it was very nice. I then had food, I had a sandwich and crisps and a strawberry yogurt.

Thea Stevens (6)

Hethersett Woodside Primary & Nursery School, Hethersett

Dear Diary

I went to the zoo with my mum and dad to buy a pet dragon and pet tiger. I jumped on the dragon's back and was racing the tiger home. We were flying and he was running through the jungle! We won. The tiger had to cook the dinner because he lost. The dragon helped to light the barbecue fire outside when he sneezed. For pudding, the dragon's fire made us toasted marshmallows with his fire breath.
It was a yummy dinner and the best day ever!

Maven Ngo-Hamilton (6)
Hydesville Tower School, Walsall

Dear Diary

Today, I went to the Amazon rainforest with my pet dinosaur. Me and my dinosaur went to swing on the green vines but then I injured my leg! Luckily, a chameleon came with a furry plant called Lamb's Ear. Eventually, it healed my small leg. After that, we went to play in a hot waterfall. Soon, it became dark. I went to shore and took off my soggy clothes and then built a den out of giant leaves.

Chevéyo Kadii Ngo-Hamilton (7)

Hydesville Tower School, Walsall

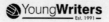

Dear Diary

I went to the park in my space rocket, and my mummy, daddy, sister and brother were spinning so fast on the roundabout. Then it turned into a spaceship and we went flying like super boys and super girls!
It was the best adventure.

Cataléya Ngo-Hamilton (5)
Hydesville Tower School, Walsall

My Fairy

Dear Diary,

It has been the weirdest day ever. I was so freaked out by it all. The strangest thing was it was weird because I was playing and I saw a magic pathway behind a tree. I nervously followed it. It led me to a magical forest where there was glitter everywhere. I could see creatures like birds, hedgehogs, ladybirds and fairies! I felt so happy to see the fairies because I never thought I would see them in my life. One fairy led me to a magical little fairy cottage. I found a magical wand that was locked up in a box, that the fairy needed. Behind the cupboard was a lock picker, so I opened the box and the fairy felt amazed. Then I followed the pathway back home.

I know what you are thinking... I didn't ask for a wish. See, a fairy was already a wish come true.

Harper Eagles (7)
Pennyhill Primary School, West Bromwich

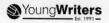
The Mysterious Island

Dear Diary,
You wouldn't guess what happened today! I am so proud of myself. I was at the beach, it was a hot afternoon, so I decided to go for a swim to cool me down. As I swam deeper and deeper, I could see a dark blue hole. I swam towards it, thinking it would take me to a fun place. It took me to a magical ice land where I could see blue crystals. There were guards everywhere. I saw a gigantic throne with a tall man sitting on it. He had icy-blue eyes and icicles on his spiky hair. There was a sign that said *No Strangers*. This made me feel terrified because I wasn't supposed to be there. I hid behind a cupboard made from ice. Then a guard saw me. I ran but the boss found me! My heart started to pound, the boss locked me in an ice cage. Would I go home? The ice boss came and I wasn't the boy he wasn't

looking for. He unlocked the door, I wouldn't move in case it was a trick.
He waved his hand and I was back in my house.

Abdulla Abdow (7)

Pennyhill Primary School, West Bromwich

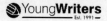

The Portals

Dear Diary,
The scariest thing happened today. I am still shaking with fear. I was playing with my toy rocket in my bedroom. Suddenly, a dark portal appeared and I went through it nervously. I took a few steps and my foot slipped. I started falling down, down, down. I felt so scared because it felt like I was falling from the sky. I fell onto the hard ground, I looked up and I was in the woods. There were lots of tall trees. I could hear something growling and I could smell something bad. I turned around and saw Grizzly bears staring at me! I felt uncomfortable. I ran as fast as I could and I could feel my heart beating fast.
I reached another portal and ran straight through it. I was so scared. The portal took me to the Atlantic Ocean. I swam. I got chased by some sharks but I swam so fast that I reached the last portal and I went

through it, and it took me home. I was so glad I was home.

Finley Bowen (7)
Pennyhill Primary School, West Bromwich

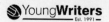

The Magic Adventure

Dear Diary,

I was walking home today and, all of a sudden, I saw a trail of sparkles on the footpath. This made me feel so excited because I thought it would lead me to a fairy. At the end of the trail, I saw an amazing, shiny, pink unicorn. Its wings were covered in glitter and its horn had lots of hearts on it. I gave the unicorn some rainbow cake because it was hungry. Then I sat on the unicorn's back, feeling joyful. I was looking forward to flying with the unicorn and seeing the whole city. We flew so high that I touched the fluffy clouds. I even tasted them and they tasted like cotton candy! I was so surprised. Next, I saw more unicorns flying and some sleeping on the clouds. Suddenly, they woke up and played with me.

I had to go back home. *Poof!* I was at home with a little help from the unicorns. Diary, it was a magical adventure.

Palak Rani (7)

Pennyhill Primary School, West Bromwich

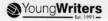
Trapped In Space

Dear Diary,
I had the craziest day *ever* in all my life! I would call this day 'Wow!'. I was in space and there were aliens everywhere. I was scared. My eyes opened wide as I saw all the strange creatures coming close to me. They started to bite my leg. I screamed but that did not help. I was thrown on my face in front of the space king. He shouted at me, "What are you doing here?" I was so scared, Diary. I did not think I would return to Earth. He locked me in a room and tried to change me into a monster! It didn't work because I was a girl from Earth. I had supergirl power and I used it to kick the door down. I felt powerful and strong. The creatures were coming to attack me but I flew in the air above them and headed for Earth.

I will never go back to that crazy place again!
Your friend,
Elizabete.

Elizabete Kravale (7)

Pennyhill Primary School, West Bromwich

Heaven

Dear Diary,

I had an unbelievable dream. Someone pushed me into a sinkhole. Strangely, it led to Heaven. All of the angels and God were there to greet me. I could not stop staring below me because I could see Earth and space. Suddenly, a magical door opened and I was called into Heaven. I was excited and nervous. Would I see God? Would I get back home to my mother and father? There was a bright light that shone from God. Then a great big voice said, "Mandla, you have one wish. What will your wish be?" I shouted loudly, "I wish COVID-19 would stop forever!"

I woke up in bed and the news reporter said no one will ever have COVID-19, for the rest of eternity. I thanked God for granting my

wish. I told you, Diary, it was an unbelievable dream. Was it really a dream? Your special friend,
Mandla.

Mandla Dhlamini
Pennyhill Primary School, West Bromwich

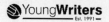

Meeting The Queen

Dear Diary,
This is what happened to make my day the strangest and craziest day in all my life...
I can't believe I was chosen for this fabulous day with Queen Elizabeth! I looked beautiful for my afternoon tea with Her Majesty. We sat for tea and I was nervous and my hands were shaking. I didn't mean to, but I spilt the tea on my dress. The mean servant shouted at me and removed me from in front of the Queen. I felt really bad and started to cry. The Queen heard my screaming and asked me to come back. She said it was okay and that I shouldn't cry. She ordered the servant to change me into a beautiful dress. When I was dressed lovely, I went back to the Queen, and she gave me a tiara and said I was now Princess Darcie.

This was the best day ever!
Your friend,
Princess Darcie.

Darcie Hunter (7)

Pennyhill Primary School, West Bromwich

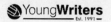
On My Way To A Scary Adventure

Dear Diary,

I have to tell you what happened this morning. You would not be able to imagine what had occurred. I was playing on the swings in the park when out of the bushes came a creature the size of an elephant and it had wings as large as buildings! I was so frightened that I fell off the wings and had a large cut forming on my knee. I was screaming because of the pain and that I was so scared. The beast began to come towards me, showing its razor-sharp teeth! I felt myself being lifted off the ground and thrown in the air. I came tumbling down onto the ground with a bump. I could feel my heart beating fast, I was so scared. I could hear the beast coming closer. All I thought of was that I wanted to get away.

I got up and ran so fast home. See, told you you would never believe me.

Shubdeep Singh (7)

Pennyhill Primary School, West Bromwich

Queen Bee

Dear Diary,
You won't believe me if when I tell you. I was picked up by a huge buzzing bee! I wouldn't believe me either, but guess what? It happened. It all started off as a normal day at the park, walking along a grassy path. I could hear the soft bubbling stream in the distance and the buzzing of bees collecting pollen. The sun was beaming bright, so bright I had to close my eyes. Out of nowhere, I felt something push me to the ground. I could hear a loud buzzing sound. Its big legs wrapped around me and the bee took me to a huge beehive! There were millions of bees making honey. The queen bee was the biggest bee there. It was wearing a golden crown as bright as the sun. I slipped in sticky honey and slid out of the hive, tumbling down my chimney.

Cameron Lane (7)
Pennyhill Primary School, West Bromwich

My Strange Adventure

Dear Diary,

Today, I woke up and I was not in my bed. I was so confused. I looked up and saw flying, pretty, cuddly teddy bears! I just wanted to see how fluffy they were. So, I ran to hug one and, yes, it was so cuddly and soft. There was a table made of sweets which had yummy colourful cupcakes on it. They looked so irresistible that I had to try one. I ran speedily towards them. One had my name sprinkled on it! I took a big bite. It was the most delicious thing I have ever tried.

Suddenly, my belly started to feel weird... A crown appeared on my head and my clothes magically changed into a beautiful dress. I was a queen! Then I rubbed my eyes and... *poof!* I was back in my bed. I thought it was a dream but it was not.

Manjot Malhi (7)

Pennyhill Primary School, West Bromwich

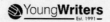

Aarif And The Magician

Dear Diary,
Sorry I haven't spoken to you in a while, I just needed time to figure out what I have just witnessed. My mum surprised me with tickets to see the greatest magician to walk the Earth! Queueing up amongst excited people, we waited to be seated. My heart began to race as if a drum in a concert. I sat down and, looking around me, all I could see were flashing lights. The curtains were raised and stood in front of me was this magician pointing directly at me. I was called onto the stage. He put me into a box and turned me into a pig, and made me teleport into a jungle! I was chased by hungry predators right in front of me and

they turned me into a goat! Then I ran into a tree.
Then I suddenly turned back into a human.

Aarif Olaniyi (7)
Pennyhill Primary School, West Bromwich

Alien Adventure

Dear Diary,

I have had the strangest day ever in my life. I went to space. You might not believe me but I did! This is what happened...

When I got there, I saw weird aliens, and the master called me and put me in a lava cage! They gave me worms, bugs and ants to eat. Strangely, they were delicious. However, I was worried for my life because I thought they were going to turn me into an evil zombie. I prayed for help over and over. Suddenly, Neil Armstrong came and saw me praying. He told me to follow him to his rocket. We ran as fast as we could to his rocket. The aliens attacked the rocket we

were in! However, we got away from the strongest aliens in space.
Your friend,
Colt.

Colt Bates (7)

Pennyhill Primary School, West Bromwich

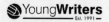
My Alien Friend

Dear Diary,

I had the weirdest day *ever*. There were aliens and they took me into their spaceship! The mother locked me in an alien jail. I was terrified and worried that I would never return to Earth. I had a visitor who became my own alien friend. His name was Boggy. We tried to steal the key but were caught. They put us in the same jail and together we escaped. We headed for my spaceship. All the aliens started to chase after us! Boggy stopped for them to catch him instead of me. I got away in my spaceship. I was sad because I left my alien friend behind, but I was happy to safe.

Diary, would you like to come with me on my next adventure?
Your friend,
Aayush Patel.

Patel Aayush (7)

Pennyhill Primary School, West Bromwich

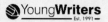

Me And The Lion

Dear Diary,
The weirdest thing happened to me last night. You would never believe it; there, stood right in front of me, was a huge lion! His thick heavy trail dragged along behind it, his round eyes followed me like spotlights. I tried not to make a sound, however, it didn't stop him from opening his mouth wide where I could see his glistening white, sharp teeth. I ran down the steps, the lion fell down the stairs. He was tumbling down. I helped the lion up, he was nice to me. Then my mum came back. I tried to hide the lion, then he was moving. My mum found the lion! I begged my mum to keep him, then my mum said yes.
Goodbye from me and the lion.

Jaya Madhar (7)
Pennyhill Primary School, West Bromwich

When I Got Dragged Up A Mountain

Dear Diary,

You won't believe where I have been today. I couldn't believe my eyes. I felt like I was standing amongst the clouds! I was sitting in the car with my parents when, all of a sudden, our car was lifted up high and we were driving up a huge mountain! It felt like something out of a movie. Then, all of a sudden, we stopped. We were surrounded by white soft snow, it felt so magical. I looked up and saw a white snowy polar bear running towards me and it was roaring like a lion! It grabbed me and took me to a deep dark cave. It was cold, my body was shaking. I found a pickaxe and mined out of the cave.

Logan Jones (7)
Pennyhill Primary School, West Bromwich

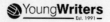
The Robots

Dear Diary,
Listen up, something crazy happened to me today. I was captured by a huge mechanical beast that towered over me. I was awakened in the middle of the night by sounds of beeping. Rubbing my eyes, I shuffled down my bed. I felt something, a tight grip around my wrist. It was cold and sharp. I was being whisked away down the hallway, dragged down the stairs and out of my front door! I was trying to smash its hand but it wouldn't let me go. He took me to a basement full of robots.
When the robots were asleep, I tried to run out. Quietly, I went on my tiptoes and snuck out.

Emily Wang (7)
Pennyhill Primary School, West Bromwich

Aliens

I had the craziest thing happen to me yesterday. I fell down a giant hole! I was terrified because I wasn't sure where I was going.

I was running from aliens and I fell over and they grabbed me. I was locked in a horrible dark cave and I was very frightened. I was locked up for twenty-six days. I was fed bugs and water! I was angry. I asked myself, *will I ever get out?* One of the alien guards one night opened the door and showed me an escape route home.

I was very happy to get home.
Your friend, Ethan.

Ethan Guo (7)

Pennyhill Primary School, West Bromwich

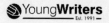
Strike Back

Dear Diary,
I was walking home from the shop.
Suddenly, I saw a giant pool of slime on the
road. I went and checked it out. I knew
exactly where this came from. It came from
the one-eyed sheep-herding monster! I had
read Roald Dahl's book about it. It tried to
defeat me, but that didn't happen. I
destroyed it with one hit, using my fist. This
made me feel good because I felt strong
and confident.
You should have seen me in action; I
thought I had superpower.

Dominic Holder (7)
Pennyhill Primary School, West Bromwich

Dear Diary

Yesterday, I went to the beach. On the beach, I built a sandcastle. After that, my mom said, "Let's do some art." Next, I went into the sea with my mom and I saw a mermaid. The mermaid had pink lips, a tail, a crown and red hair. After that, I ate a burger, then we had a picnic. Next, me and my sister played games. After that, I went into the water by myself and I started swimming.
Next, I went home and I was exhausted.

Sorana-Nicoleta Capiau (6)
Pennyhill Primary School, West Bromwich

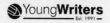

Dear Diary

Today was great! I went to London with my mommy, daddy and my sister, Lisbeth. We went by car, it took two hours. We saw a fountain, it had grey lions and they were huge. Next, we went on the London Eye. We felt excited because we were so high. We could see for miles, it was amazing.
After that, we went to a cafe and had some yummy food before going home.

Rosie Butler (5)
Pennyhill Primary School, West Bromwich

Dear Diary

I had an amazing day! I went to London with my best friend, Ella. I went on a train and it took forever. We went on the London Eye. I felt scared because we were so high. We could see for miles. It was amazing. Next, we went to get some yummy chips. Finally, we went home and I went to bed. Speak soon.

Scarlett-Mae Hughes (6)
Pennyhill Primary School, West Bromwich

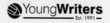

Dear Diary

Today was the best day of my life!
I went to London with a blue monster called
Ariyun. We got there in a rocket, it was
super fast. We went to Trafalgar Square
and we saw a fountain. On the fountain,
there were huge grey lions.
We went home, I was so tired.
Love, Kyrun.

Kyrun Bali (6)
Pennyhill Primary School, West Bromwich

Dear Diary

I had the best day ever!
I went to London with my mommy and daddy, and we went on a rainbow bus. It took us two hours. We saw Big Ben, it was tall and loud. Next, we went on the London Eye. It was amazing.
Finally, we went home.
Love from Shamiya.

Shamiya Barrett (6)
Pennyhill Primary School, West Bromwich

Dear Diary

Yesterday, I went through a secret tunnel. It was dark and it was scary. There was a creepy doll and I went with my family. After that, I got out and I went to the funfair. I saw a unicorn, it looked like a mermaid. I went back home, I was exhausted.

Amrita Shergill
Pennyhill Primary School, West Bromwich

Dear Diary

Today was amazing!
The Queen came to our school for a tea party.
To protect the Queen from the virus, we washed our hands and we kept our distance. At our party, we listened to music and we had cake and squash.
Speak soon,
Love, Riza.

Riza Nayeem (6)
Pennyhill Primary School, West Bromwich

Dear Diary

Today was amazing. The Queen came to our school and we had a tea party with the Queen. We had some delicious squash and some fresh cake. Then we listened to some lovely music.
To keep safe, we kept our distance.
Speak soon,
Love from Reuben xx

Reuben Fuery (5)
Pennyhill Primary School, West Bromwich

Dear Diary

Today was amazing. We had a tea party with the Queen. We had some delicious squash and some fresh cake. Then we listened to some lovely music. I felt proud because I met Her Majesty, Queen Elizabeth the II.
Speak soon,
Love, Nihaal xx

Kawar Naunihaal Singh (6)
Pennyhill Primary School, West Bromwich

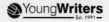

Dear Diary

I went to the funfair and got on the trampoline. I went to the funfair with my mum and dad, my sister and brother. I went on the slide and I was very excited. The slide was big and I liked going down.
It was a lovely day.

Phoebe Wall Boateng (6)
Pennyhill Primary School, West Bromwich

Dear Diary

Today was amazing. We had a tea party with the Queen. We had some delicious squash and some fresh cake. Then we listened to lovely music.
I felt happy because I met the Queen.
Speak soon,
Love, Agata xx

Agata Puzyrkiewicz (6)
Pennyhill Primary School, West Bromwich

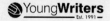

Dear Diary

I went to the funfair with my mommy, daddy and my brother. I went on the swings because I wanted a go. It was fun. I was swinging very high.
After that, we went home. I had a good day.
Bye,
Maddison.

Maddison Turner (6)
Pennyhill Primary School, West Bromwich

Dear Diary

Today, I went to the park with a dragon!
The dragon was black and his name was
End Dragon. He was big and he had a long
tail. We went down the slide. The slide was
long and shiny.
Then we both went home.

Oliver Stanislawski (6)
Pennyhill Primary School, West Bromwich

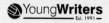

Dear Diary

Today was wonderful because we had a
lovely day at our tea party with the Queen.
At the party, we had some squash and cake.
I would love it if you came.
Speak soon,
Rachel Morrison.

Rachel Morrison (6)
Pennyhill Primary School, West Bromwich

Dear Diary

Today was amazing because the Queen came to our school for a tea party.
To keep safe from COVID, we washed our hands and we kept our distance.
Speak soon,
Love from Imaan xoxo

Imaan Olaniyi (6)
Pennyhill Primary School, West Bromwich

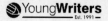

Dear Diary

Today was amazing because the Queen came to our class, and we had some delicious squash and fresh cake.
Then we listened to some lovely music and I felt proud because I met the Queen.

Toluwanimi Eniolorunda (6)
Pennyhill Primary School, West Bromwich

Dear Diary

Today, I went to the park.
I went with a fairy. The fairy was friendly. I was excited because I wanted to go on the slide. The slide was tall and shiny.
After that, I went home.

Jessica Garrity (6)
Pennyhill Primary School, West Bromwich

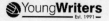

Dear Diary

Today was an amazing day because we had fresh squash and nice cake.
After that, we listened to some lovely music.
Speak soon,
Love, Leo.

Leo Bolinski (6)

Pennyhill Primary School, West Bromwich

Dear Diary

Today, I went to the beach with my friend, Ellis. We were walking on the sand and suddenly a sand monster came out of the sand! We walked to the monster and became friends. On the beach we played monster baseball and the ball was a star shape. We all went swimming in the sea. We swam to an island and we found a treasure chest, and inside there was a pizza and ice cream! The monster went like this "Yum, yum!" and rubbed his belly. Me and Ellis laughed. We got a boat and went back to the beach. A cheeky, greedy seagull took my ice cream! The sand monster laughed and Ellis said "Hey, come back here!" We got back to the beach, then the monster dried out. He crumbled to the floor. I said, "Aww, he was lots of fun!"
I hope he is there next time.

Adam O'Doherty (7)
St Stephen's Kearsley Moor CE Primary School, Kearsley

Dear Diary

14th June 2020
You will not believe what happened yesterday, I'm a big sister! I was nervous but excited. My auntie came for a sleepover and I helped her put the decorations up.
I made my own Wonder Woman outfit. I was shy and happy. There were balloons and a message and flowers for when my mummy and baby sister came home.
My dad told me to get ready. I made my own Wonder Woman outfit, it was red, blue and yellow. I was feeling nervous in the car. When we got there I saw my baby sister she was really cute. We got home, Mum was surprised. She was so happy. We took photos. We had a lovely time.
From Jasmine. Xx

Jasmine Sheikh (7)
St Stephen's Kearsley Moor CE Primary School, Kearsley

Dear Diary

Today, I walked to the football field with my friend Finley and our dads. We took a football and a large-sized net. We practised our power-shooting penalities, our left-foot strikes, our dribbling skills and our free-kicks. It was fun. I love playing football, it is the best thing in the world!
Then I had a lovely tasty pizza, then we watched a movie and I went to bed at 10pm.

Ethan Fox (7)

St Stephen's Kearsley Moor CE Primary School, Kearsley

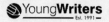
Dear Diary

Me and my friend went to space! We played football games, then my friend sneezed out slime and it went everywhere. Then a monster jumped out and scared us! After that, we painted on the moon with green smelly slime. Then we got back into the rocket, then we nearly crashed into green fat aliens and we nearly crashed into farms. Then we got home.

Finley Pendlebury (6)
St Stephen's Kearsley Moor CE Primary School, Kearsley

Dear Diary

Last week, I was walking down the road when I saw two superheroes. They came over to me and said, "Do you want to come to tea?"
"Yes!" I said. I came to their base, they had amazing gadgets. We played lots of fun games and one of the superheroes picked me up and threw me!

Paige Jones (7)

St Stephen's Kearsley Moor CE Primary School, Kearsley

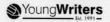

Dear Diary

Today, I went to Wonder Park. All the rides were phenomenal. I love my magic pen because it can make any ride in the world. When I go there, I'm very happy.
My spirits lifted when I was there and I met the wonder in Wonder Park who created it, June.

Teegan Thompson (7)
St Stephen's Kearsley Moor CE Primary School, Kearsley

Dear Diary

I went to the funfair with a caring fairy. We went on a fun ride, then we won a teddy. After, we went to a cafe. We ate a yummy cupcake.
After that, we had a sleepover at my house. We had a pillow fight, then we went to bed.

Lara Al Muqdadi (7)
St Stephen's Kearsley Moor CE Primary School, Kearsley

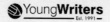

Dear Diary

I went to the funfair and it was fun.
I love my family so much. My best friends
are Ella and Alice, and we are BFFs. I like
superheroes because they save the day.
I went to the park with my friends and it
was fun.

Esme Thomasson (6)

St Stephen's Kearsley Moor CE Primary School,
Kearsley

Dear Diary

Today, we went to the park with my best friends, my family and my horse called Lucy. Me and my best friend, Esraa, went on the big, big, big slide, and Kensi went on the swing.
We had the best, best of times.

Kaylee Ann Robinson (7)
St Stephen's Kearsley Moor CE Primary School, Kearsley

Dear Diary

Today, I went to the funfair. I went with my family.
At the fair, we saw a dinosaur horse riding and dancing! We ate a picnic outside and played football before we came home.

Elijah Hayton (7)
St Stephen's Kearsley Moor CE Primary School, Kearsley

Dear Diary

Dear Diary,

Today was the most amazing day ever.

It all started when I woke up early and because of this, I am so tired. My best friend threw a sleepy potion at me and then we went downstairs. I went to the Nether and found some breakfast, then I went mining. I love it in the Nether. When I got to my strip-mine, I could not go any further because of a pig. My best friend showed up and killed the pig so I could carry on. Suddenly, Herobrine unleashed a swarm of bees! Luckily, I killed them all.

I was so tired I kept falling asleep, so I went home with my best friend and went to bed.

Johni Ashenden (6)

The Priors School, Priors Marston

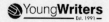

Dear Diary

Dear Diary,

Today was weird because I woke up and it was the end of the world, so I decided to mine for a very special crystal called Netherite. I started mining and mining until I got to Bedrock! Then I saw some Netherite but... there was a guard blocking it. I went down into the cave and an arrow hit me. It hurt a lot, so I blew fire at the guard and got the Netherite. I returned to Ghost Island with all my ghost friends. There was Sad Ghost, Angry Ghost, Worried Ghost and loads more emotions.

My favourite is Funky Ghost. He plays all the music and he was also on his 9th grade of DJing. My least favourite ghost is Worried Ghost because, as you can imagine, he is always worried and scared. He is even scared of a clock. Silly old Worried Ghost.

We had our tea and supper and then went to sleep, waiting for another great day.

Arthur Jaques (6)
The Priors School, Priors Marston

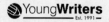

Dear Diary

Dear Diary,
Today, I woke up and I felt weird but then I remembered that it was my birthday! I felt *sooo* happy because I knew my mum was taking me to the park. I was flying my kite when, suddenly, it flew away. I ran into the woods to find it but then I got lost. I heard a noise and a person named Amy took me home. I felt so happy and I said thank you to Amy.
My mum said to Amy that she can visit whenever she likes.

Pippa Hewins (6)
The Priors School, Priors Marston

Dear Diary

Dear Diary,

Today was a super weird day.

I went on a boat trip but I got lost and ended up on this weird island. I had to build a shelter. I got a bit scared because there were lots of bombs. I looked in the forest and I found a new boat. I used the boat to go home.

When I got home, I felt safe again and I told my mummy the whole story.

Ivy Wingrove (6)

The Priors School, Priors Marston

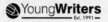

Dear Diary

Dear Diary,
My name is DustyPaprika408. I was playing 'Dogtopia' and I turned myself into a dog. But then my sister joined the game and she banned blocks. I broke the 'command' block and I felt so happy. Then I went on the doggy plane but it crashed!
I found another one and flew home to my dog house.

Jarvis Owen (6)
The Priors School, Priors Marston

Dear Diary

Dear Diary,

Today was a great day!

I woke up and I woke my owner. She jumped, so I ran down the stairs and then we went to the park. I met Ruffalls and we played fetch together. When my owner threw the ball into the bush, we ran away and got lost.

Soon, we found our way home again.

Eliza Parratt (7)

The Priors School, Priors Marston

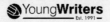
Dear Diary

Dear Diary,
Today was a great day! I went to the ship to fight the rebels but Baby Yoda was there, so I brought in the Stormtroopers. They were shooting but Baby Yoda was blocking the bullets.
Then Darth Maul snatched Baby Yoda and I went back to the ship.

Elias Barlow (6)
The Priors School, Priors Marston

Dear Diary

Dear Diary,

Today was a wonderful day in Minecraft.
I teleported to the Nether and looked for Netherite. But while I was looking, Piglin spotted me, so I got my bow and arrow and I shot it.
I teleported back to the normal world and went to bed.

Henry Roberts (6)

The Priors School, Priors Marston

Dear Diary

Dear Diary,
Today was a really good day.
We went to the park and I went on the swing. The first thing I did was play on the swing and then a lion came to frighten me! It had escaped from the zoo.
I screamed and ran all the way home.

Immy Threlfall (6)
The Priors School, Priors Marston

Dear Diary

Dear Diary,
Today was superb. It was Sunday morning when I woke up in a mess! I zoomed into the kitchen and I looked around. There was Izzy, my owner. Izzy said something about the park, so I ran to the door. Izzy opened it and we went.

Freya Van Vuuren (6)

The Priors School, Priors Marston

Dear Diary

Dear Diary,
Today was a horrible day.
I went to the forest and I saw three pigs. I was hungry and I wanted to eat them. I blew their houses down but the brick house was too strong.
I went down the chimney and then burnt my bottom!

Tilly Barron (6)
The Priors School, Priors Marston

Dear Diary

Dear Diary,

Today was very exciting. The wind was howling when I woke up. It was very early. I looked over at my mirror and I saw that I was a wolf! I tried to get myself back and soon I realised that everything was back to normal.

Cora Sadler (6)

The Priors School, Priors Marston

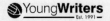

Dear Diary

Dear Diary,
Today I went to the Batcave. I was parking my Batmobile when I saw that there was slime on the path. It was Killercroc. I got Robin to catch Killercroc, but then Joker escaped.
I was angry because Joker escaped!

Archie Cox (7)
The Priors School, Priors Marston

Dear Diary

I took off in my green robot lion! I know what you're thinking; where am I going to find food and water? Where am I going to go?

The planet is called Altaya! It is a very, very beautiful place. It has flowers and a princess called Alora, a butler called Coran, and there are five lions that can turn into a ginormous robot! And there are pilots called Paladines.

Aurora Jackson-Hamilton (7)
Tongue Primary School, Lairg

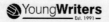

Dear Diary

I wanted to go to space. So, I got on my space turbo board and I was off!
I landed on a planet. I did not know what planet I was on but I was on Mars! I could tell it was Mars because it was red!
I found two flamingoes. I helped them dig for water but it was very hard!

Mia Martin (7)
Tongue Primary School, Lairg

Dear Diary

I will blast off on my *mega chicken!* I will go to the planet Uranus to eat Uranus bananas. The bananas I eat will change my body forever, in a good way. I will be able to breathe in space.

I hate green aliens! I can eat rocks, I can turn rocks into cotton candy.

Ruaridh Faccenda (7)
Tongue Primary School, Lairg

Dear Diary

I am going with my dad, I am going in a space rocket. I am going to Saturn in my rocket. We are going to have a picnic with ham wraps, Dunkers and juice.
We will do some exploring and maybe find a space diamond.

Magnus Holmes (7)
Tongue Primary School, Lairg

Dear Diary

I am going to the moon with Rana, Mum and Dad. We are going on a pterodactyl and it is going to be fast!
When I get to the moon, I am going to play with my friend, Everest, and have a picnic.

Lars Rueben Mackay-Buttress (5)

Tongue Primary School, Lairg

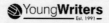

Dear Diary

I took off on my flying stairs!
I am Struan Scientist. Mummy was driving
the flying stairs. I landed on the cheesy
moon and shrank it to eat it.
Mega Stairs took us home again.

Struan Mackay-Shanks (6)

Tongue Primary School, Lairg

Dear Diary

I am going to space in my flying house. My friend, Elli, is going to come with me and we are going to have a birthday party with a magical unicorn!

Olivia Findlay (5)
Tongue Primary School, Lairg

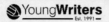

Dear Diary

I was going to the moon in a rocket.
The journey was super fast and very bumpy.
When I got to the moon, I had a picnic with
a unicorn and an alien!

Lucy Mackay (6)
Tongue Primary School, Lairg

Dear Diary

I am going to Planet Mars on my pet dragon.
I am going to meet my space sisters! We are going to have a picnic with smoothies and sweets.

Elli Scott (5)

Tongue Primary School, Lairg

Dear Diary

I went to the moon on a seadragon. A green alien came with me. She was eating jelly. We were jumping on the moon and went really high.

Paige Jones (6)
Tongue Primary School, Lairg

Young Writers
Information

We hope you have enjoyed reading this book – and
that you will continue to in the coming years.

If you're a young writer who enjoys reading and creative
writing, or the parent of an enthusiastic poet or story writer,
visit our website **www.youngwriters.co.uk/subscribe** to join
the World of Young Writers and receive news, competitions,
writing challenges, tips, articles and giveaways! There
is lots to keep budding writers motivated to write!

If you would like to order further copies of this book,
or any of our other titles, then please give us a
call or order via your online account.

Young Writers
Remus House
Coltsfoot Drive
Peterborough
PE2 9BF
(01733) 890066
info@youngwriters.co.uk

Join in the conversation!
Tips, news, giveaways and much more!

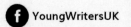 YoungWritersUK   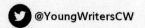 @YoungWritersCW   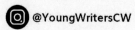 @YoungWritersCW